AFTER I FALL

A FALLING NOVEL

JESSICA SCOTT

AFTER I FALL
The Falling Series

Her entire life has been a lie. Being with Eli is the most honest thing she's ever done.

Parker Hauser lives the perfect life and knows exactly where she's been and where she's going. Parker has to be perfect. Perfect grades, perfect body, perfect life.

Until she meets Eli Winter.

Eli throws her entire life into chaos when he denies her the one thing she wants from him.

One chance encounter stokes her desire for the man who refused to touch her and left her questioning everything.

When Parker tries to help his new business, the spotlight turns on Eli's military record. And the war he's tried to forget may destroy them both.

THE FALLING SERIES
Before I Fall: Noah & Beth
Break My Fall: Abby & Josh
After I Fall: Parker & Eli
Catch My Fall: Deacon & Kelsey

Note – these books are fiction. Any resemblance to real people or events is purely coincidence

Learn More At…
http://www.jessicascott.net
Follow Jessica on Twitter
Like Jessica on Facebook
Sign up for Jessica's Newsletter

Printed in the United States of America

First Printing 2017

ISBN: 978-1-942102-19-9

Author photo courtesy of Buzz Covington Photography

Cover Photo courtesy of Krause Photography

Cover design by Jessica Scott

For more information please see www.jessicascott.net

To Kame & Pat
For being there from the beginning

AFTER I FALL

CHAPTER 1

Parker

My day doesn't always start with dicks, but when it does, they are usually unsolicited and where my supposed fiancé can find them. Like it's my fault they show up, somehow.

"Stupid dick pic."

Muttering to myself as I cross campus isn't really normal behavior for me. But today, well, today has crossed the line into completely abnormal.

And yes, that means I have seen more than one unsolicited—and often rather sad and pathetic—penis arrive in my inbox. I'm really not sure what makes men think that random women will be impressed by their wildly disappointing penises.

None of the pics are ever anything to write home about. Not that unsolicited penis is *ever* something to brag about. But seriously. Do they all have to be so mediocre?

The latest iteration looks like a plucked baby chickadee that fell out of its nest. If this is what I have to look forward to when I get old, you can cancel that shit.

Old dicks are gross.

Which doesn't mean I'm morally opposed to penises. On the contrary. Just not ones attached to men forty years older than I am.

"Who the hell thinks their dick is so fucking special that they send it to people out of the blue? Like 'hey, I know you're totally coming to work for me in a couple of weeks and *bam*, here's my dick. Hope you like it'."

I have exactly one week to figure out a new plan for me to get a letter for the executive management program here at the business school. Oh, and the company I was supposed to work at this summer that was going to get me an interview…well, thanks to a certain ill-timed penis arrival, that whole plan just got flushed down the toilet and went swirly.

I'm scrolling through my phone, looking at advertisements on the student website, hoping an internship will magically appear and save me from having to go home and explain this to my father.

My phone vibrates. Thankfully, it's not a dick. Well, not exactly, anyway.

Nope; instead it's my dad.

Who I also don't really want to talk to. Once upon a time, I would have asked him for help but, well, Dad hasn't really been all there since my mom died six years ago.

My dad's going to ask me about the internship, and I don't have any answers. At least, not any that he's prepared to listen to.

Hey, Dad, there's this dick I need to talk to you about.

How's that for a nonstarter for a conversation? My life would be so different if I had a father who didn't love my fiancé like the son he always wanted more than the daughter who was marrying the future son-in-law.

I reach beneath my sunglasses and rub my eyes, fighting the burning tears. How did everything get so colossally fucked up?

"Are you okay?"

I look up, surprised at the unexpected concern from an unfamiliar voice. The woman in front of me is...sharp. She's athletic and sleek, but it's the roses and thorns twisting up her arms that draw my attention. The red roses stand in stark contrast to the black and grey thorns. Her eyes are liquid gold, lined with sultry brown.

She looks just as lost as I feel at the moment.

So why she's stopped and asked if I'm okay...surprised is putting it mildly.

I paste on a blinding, well-practiced smile. "I'm fine. Thank you, though, for asking."

She narrows her eyes at me then tips her chin. "Last time I saw someone arguing with themselves like that, it didn't end well."

I pause, not really sure what to do with her standing there in front of me. I don't normally have conversations with strangers and I certainly don't introduce my mental health status in the opening interaction.

But I'm also curious. I toy with the zipper on my purse. "Um, how did it end?"

She grins and her expression shifts to something wistful, something laced with memory. It has the odd effect of making her look sharper and softer. It's an odd combination. "With me wrestling his ass to the ground and taking the crazy fuck to the fifth floor."

I lift both eyebrows, not entirely sure about what she's just said or if it's even possible for a woman to wrestle a guy to the ground, but I'm not going to be the one to find out if she's telling the truth. "Really? That's kind of badass. Like all *Xena: Warrior Princess* and stuff."

"It wasn't nearly as exciting as all that." Her voice is smooth and confident. Man, I wish I had her poise. She'd probably rip someone's dick off through the phone if they sent her an unwanted penis. And she'd know what to do when her fiancé didn't believe her when she told him where said dick came from. "You don't happen to know where the financial aid office is, do you? I've been wandering around campus for an hour."

"I think it's over near admissions," I tell her. "If you follow this road all the way out of the quad, you should walk right to it." I point her in the right direction, then glare down at my phone again.

"Hey, thanks." She folds her arms over her chest and cocks her hip. "So what's so wrong that you're running around campus bitching to yourself?" Like she expects me to just open up and lay all my problems at her feet.

I take a deep breath. Part of me, the part that's shrunk away from the world because the world sends you dick pics, the part of me that wants to run and hide, is actually reaching toward the care in her voice. Reaching out, craving...connection. A sense of belonging, to someone or something.

"I'm trying to find an internship for the summer. Mine...fell through." I don't usually have a hard time finding words, but there you have it. I can't bring myself to admit that I've been sent the image of an unwelcome sixty-year-old pecker. Davis's words are an insidious whisper in my head. *What did you do to deserve it?*

"Oh, well, you're in luck." She stuffs a sheet of paper in my hand. I look down. In bold black letters, my saving grace may have just been handed to me on a silver platter lined with tattooed roses.

Wanted: Intern. Learn about small business skills and entrepreneur-ship. Apply in person only. References must be non-family and from the last year.

My smile is hesitant. Unsure.

People just don't do things like this.

It's weird and a little...nice. I don't really know what to do with nice these days. It's in rather short supply.

"Wow, thank you so much."

"No problem." She grins and suddenly looks much, much younger. "You should come by tonight. I'll introduce you to the owner. It's salsa night and I make a mean margarita."

"You're a bartender?"

She nods and her eyes are glittering in the bright light. "Yep. Over at The Pint. I've got a few side gigs to help pay the bills." She motions toward the paper. "Seriously, come by tonight. It'll distract you from whatever else is going on. You look like you need a night out, anyway."

The paper in my hand has my salvation inscribed on it in smooth black letters. "Thanks. I think I've got plans tonight but I'll swing in tomorrow? Will the owner be there?"

"Yeah, he's always around. Like a mother hen, to be honest." But there's no venom in those words. Only a disgruntled affection that has me even more curious. I've heard people describe their bosses using many terms but mother hen isn't one of them.

"Thank you," I finally say. Because she may have seriously saved me from the most awkward conversation I never want to have.

And that, ladies and gentlemen, is the first non-frenemy female interaction I've had in years.

Miracles, it seems, might really exist.

Eli

PEOPLE ALWAYS LOOK at me like I've got a dick growing out of my forehead when I tell them I miss the Army. 'Course, I suppose I have to consider my audience these days. I'm not bouncing at Ropers out in Harker Heights anymore or dragging drunk GIs out of that esteemed institution. No, my life at Fort Hood is long gone.

The dirt parking lot at Ropers was filled with F-150s and Dodge Rams, complete with truck nuts and NRA stickers. The cars here are valet-parked in a lot around the corner and out of sight. They are Mercedes' and BMWs with the occasional McLaren thrown in.

It's about as far from Fort Hood as I can possibly get, at least culturally. You wouldn't think I was still even in the South with how different things are here.

I suppose there are worse problems to have than dealing with rich dicks who buy the top-shelf liquor and run up five-hundred-dollar tabs in a few hours' worth of drinking.

They keep my business in the black, so I don't really have any reason to complain. Especially when my other customer base likes to start bar fights as though we *were* back at Ropers.

Which is why, at the moment, I have a former West Point officer squared up with a business school escapee and they're getting ready to start breaking furniture if me or Deacon don't step in. Like now.

I'm standing in the shadows, looking out at my bar. My place. My merry band of misfit toys. Every one of us is a refugee from civilian life, desperately reaching out to our small circle of veterans just to feel fucking *normal*.

Deacon is behind the counter, doing his thing with a dark-haired girl with perky tits and an ass just made for gripping. And Kelsey Ryder is clueless as ever that he'd drop everything for her. I grin as she slaps him on the ass with a bar towel. The crowd eats it up.

Out of everyone in my fucked-up little tribe, Deacon is probably the most normal, despite everything he's been through. Or at least he's the most honest about it. He drinks when the bad times come; he fucks hard when they're gone. His dick is probably going to fall off one of these days, but one thing he's never done is tried to pretend that everything is honky-fucking-dory.

I scrub my hand over my beard.

Deacon knows more about the area than I ever will, and I've been using the shit out of him to navigate local politics as I try to grow The Pint's position and stature in the community. It's tricky down here in the South, and even though I'm not exactly unconnected, the connections I do have I don't want to call in.

He catches me in the shadows and wanders over. "What are you moping about tonight?" Subtle as always.

"Not moping. Contemplating life choices," I mutter.

He lifts one eyebrow and continues to wipe down glasses, stacking them on a towel near the ice. "You could have fooled me. It very much looks like you're moping."

I shrug. Deacon will see what Deacon wants to see, and nothing I say will change that. It's better not to argue with him, especially when he's actually right.

"Let's just say recent events have got me rethinking what's really important."

I look out at the bar in time to see Kelsey taking a shot off the bar with just her mouth. "Yeah, we've got a real family element here."

"It might be more *Addams Family* than *Leave it to Beaver* but it's still a family. And maybe I've realized that there are some things more important in life than a good paycheck."

I jerk my chin toward Caleb and some guy who is wearing clothes far too expensive for a bar like The Pint.

"Your turn or mine to deal with Captain Pain in the Balls?"

"Your turn."

Kelsey's rocking it behind the bar tonight. I'm glad. Sometimes, there are too many gaps between her good nights.

"You really care about your people, don't you? About us," Deacon asks, nodding in Kelsey's direction. Deacon catches me staring.

I scrub my hand over my beard once more, wishing Deacon was a little less perceptive. "What makes you say that?"

"The way you watch over us. Even someone like Caleb, who you can't stand, you still stayed at the hospital with him. There's a thousand little things you do every day to take care of people."

I shrug. "Guess I'm hardwired that way."

"What about you, though? Who takes care of you?"

I suck in a deep breath, then let it out with deliberate slowness. "As long as what I do still matters, then I'm okay."

A simple, uncomplicated truth.

I slide a bottle of tequila over to Deacon. "Guess it's my turn to break up the fight tonight?"

Deacon grins and slaps me on the back. "You know I'm on probation from the last one. I'd prefer not to spend the last week of classes hoping you can hit up a GoFundMe to bail my ass out of jail."

I touch the tips of my fingers to my brow in a mock salute. "Touché."

Bracing myself, I wade into the argument between Caleb, the resident pain in my ass who has recently refused to attempt sobriety and as a result, has assumed the mantle of the person most likely to get into a bar fight, and my other customer.

Caleb is one of those guys who just rubs people the wrong way, but tonight, at least, he's not alone if he's here. Not sure how I feel about him continuing to hang out at the bar, considering he just got out of the hospital for almost drinking himself into a coma. It's pretty fucking dumb that he's here.

I don't talk about the Army much. Not with my wealthier customers, anyway. Every so often someone will notice the 82nd Airborne Division tattoo buried in the swirling black ink lines on my bicep but most people don't bother to look closely enough.

People see what they want to see. That's how Caleb found his place among the misfit Legos and toys that are drawn to The Pint. He saw a fellow veteran and started talking shit about killing 'em all and letting God sort them out and I politely told him to shut the fuck up. Which apparently endeared me to him for life because he has become a semi-permanent resident over the last year or so.

And I'm a fucking sucker, because I keep letting him come back where at least I can keep an eye on him and make sure he's not drinking himself into a coma like he did a few weeks ago.

I can't stop him.

And I can't cut him loose. No matter how much he might piss off my higher-paying customers.

It doesn't work that way.

But tonight, they're not going to see a former company commander with a life full of regrets. They're going to see a big guy with a beard and tattoos breaking up yet another bar fight.

I drag Caleb off the suit. "Out. Both of you." Caleb holds up both hands and tries to look innocent. "I don't really want to hear it."

"Oh come on! Dickless over there took my chair." Caleb's version of Veteran Outrage Syndrome is annoying on a good day. I'm not in the mood tonight.

Not that I ever am.

"Call me Dickless one more time." This from the suit wearing a pair of three-hundred-dollar Cole Haan shoes. You'd think someone with that much money wouldn't be insecure about the state of his manhood.

I sigh. Too often Caleb reminds me of all the reasons I despise my alma mater. Guys who sign up, thinking the Army is going to make them into men.

Or maybe I just loathe guys like him. He's such a fucking stereotype.

No one would ever look at me and see a West Point grad. And if Caleb doesn't settle down immediately, I'm going to confirm everyone's stereotypes about tattooed, bearded bar owners.

"Either knock this shit off or you're both gone. It's a fucking football game."

Caleb holds up his hands again and heads to the latrine. Three-Hundred-Dollar Shoes stumbles to the bar, I hope to settle up rather than keep drinking.

When someone is that far in the bag, it's no longer about having any fun or running up a tab.

Crisis averted, I head back to the bar. The news is on. Another soldier wounded in Syria. Christ, what a shitshow.

I stand there, mute, absorbing the details of the latest bombings.

I've got inventories to run and paperwork to file and drinks to pour. But instead, I'm standing behind my bar, trying to chase away the memories. Trying to forget what the news in Syria reminds me of.

Wishing that it wasn't a lie when I tell people I have no regrets about the decisions I've made. I would change everything.

I pour a double shot of tequila. In the quiet din of the corner of my bar, I raise my glass toward the TV. Just a little. I don't want to draw attention to my small tribute.

I lift the glass in silent tribute to the men who've died in this pointless war, wishing I could just drag my ass upstairs and drink myself stupid.

I catch Deacon watching me a moment before he lifts his own glass in quiet tribute. I toss back the shot and close my eyes, trying not to see, trying to ignore it. Hoping to numb the dull ache in my chest that never seems to go away. It's just some days, I'm busy enough to pretend it's not there.

He gets it. I wish he didn't. I wish Kelsey didn't carry around the scars that she did. But that's the way life goes in our little band of misfits. The war is behind us but none of us has ever really come fully home.

It's why I can't take a knee. I might not be in the Army anymore, but I can't just leave.

I have to keep going. This is my place. And there are men and women counting on me. Maybe not to protect them from bullets and bad guys. But what we have here…it's important. It matters.

Maybe if I keep telling myself that, I'll actually believe it someday.

CHAPTER 2

Parker

THERE IS BEING ALONE and there is being lonely. And sitting on the other side of a locked bathroom door, listening to my future fiancé grovel is not nearly being alone enough.

"Park, I said I was sorry. I overreacted." His voice has never grated on my nerves as much as it does right now. Maybe it's because I can still feel the bite of his fingers gouging the skin of my upper arms. "I just love you so much. I can't stand the idea of you looking at another man."

I swallow hard and lift the ice pack off my upper arm. The bruises are already red and tinged with purple. These are going to stick around a while.

I thought the fight about the dick pic was over. Boy, was I fucking wrong.

"You can leave anytime." My voice doesn't shake or tremble. He's lucky I didn't call the cops, but I don't feel like dealing with the scandal.

And it's not like they'd believe me anyway.

Besides, it's not really a big deal. It's just a couple of bruises.

"What can I do to fix this?"

Start by respecting my fucking request to leave my apartment. But I don't say that. Because it feels too much like overreacting. He's never hurt me before. Never laid a hand on me or raised his voice.

And isn't that just a sad commentary on my life right now?

"Look, none of this would have happened if you'd just been honest with me when everything went down. You have a nasty habit of lying to me, Parker. I'm sorry but I'm not going to apologize for being suspicious. If you lie about sex..."

I lean my head back on the door, looking up at the ceiling. Oh, that is so rich. I don't even know how to respond.

Six months ago, I was happy. I was engaged and working on my application for business school.

Something slams into the door, scaring the shit out of me. My heart pounds against my ribs, breaking beneath the weight of the hurt.

"Damn it, fine. Have it your way. Take a couple of days to cool off, but when I come back, we're going to talk about this. And the wedding. And the weekend at the Outer Banks with my parents that I am not cancelling." His voice twists just a little. It's sad that I notice the change now. I never noticed it before. When things were good between us. "I'm going to let you have your little tantrum. But you are not going to embarrass me in front of my parents."

There are fifteen tiles in the ceiling. "Oh, I wouldn't dream of it," I whisper.

Because no one would believe me, even if I tried. That's the way this stuff always works for girls like me, isn't it?

I finally push to my feet and look at my arm in the mirror. It's not the end of the world. He grabbed me a little too hard. It's fine.

But the bruises blur in the mirror. My eyes fill and shame

crawls around my spine, squeezing tight until I can barely breathe.

I need an out. An escape. A way to get Davis to call the whole thing off so that I don't get blamed for ruining everything I've carefully constructed since my mom died and I tried my hand at rebellion.

I don't rebel anymore. I've been practicing staying inside the lines. Trying so hard to make my father proud. To make him even notice that I exist.

If I end things with Davis, things would go back to the way they were after my mom died. The birthday cards from the secretary. The silence on the other end of the phone when I call.

The emptiness reminds me of everything I lost when my mom died. If I lose Davis, I lose my dad.

Again.

The apartment is empty when I finally leave the bathroom. I hate this feeling of being trapped. Of being useless.

I'm many things, but I'm not useless. At least not normally.

But tonight, my arm is throbbing. I need a way out. Out of this apartment. Out of the gilded cage that my life has become.

My purse is on the kitchen island, the contents shaken out across the blond marble surface.

Sighing, I start to gather my belongings.

Then I see it. Crumpled beneath the desk. The paper with the internship information on it.

I swallow, looking at the bar's letterhead. The Pint.

I don't rebel anymore. I'm a good girl. And good girls don't go to bars by themselves.

And that is fucking bullshit meant to keep us from living the life we want. Teach us how to be good and we never break the rules, never upset the status quo.

My status quo needs a little upsetting tonight, damn it.

I wrap my fingers gently around the bruises of my upper arm.

There is a faint feeling, somewhere in the vicinity of my bruised heart.

Tonight, I'm feeling a teeny spark of rebellion. And it feels… good. More than good. It feels like me, coming out of a fog. Just the idea of *doing* something feels so much more right instead of being a passive little doll.

Tomorrow, I can go back to being Davis's arm candy.

Tonight? I'm going to make some new friends.

Eli

KELSEY STROLLS IN, thirty minutes late for her shift. She tosses her purse behind the bar and immediately starts slinging drinks next to Deacon, who she apparently isn't speaking to. Again.

I refuse to get involved in whatever is going on between them. My business management instructor would probably say I need to fire some folks. My father taught me that's not how the loyalty works.

And while none of us is in the Army anymore, some lessons are hard to shake.

Besides, Kelsey is a goddess behind the bar and she's usually got a quick smile and a smart mouth on her. Tonight, though, she's a little off.

Deacon frowns in her direction, then focuses on pouring another round of Goldschlager for the sorority girl party that walked in. It's like they voted to spend some quality time in support of the local veterans' charity, aka my bar.

Which is good because that means the word is getting out about the bar.

Deacon grunts and passes the tray of drinks to one of the sorority girls. "You make any headway on getting the internship filled?"

"I told you we're not hiring an intern. We don't need the trouble of trying to train up someone new."

Kelsey leans over, topping off one of Deacon's drinks in a way that makes it clear she's correcting his pour. She's poking at him tonight. Wonder why. But I'd rather bite my tongue off than ask.

"Too late. Met a girl who's going to come in to talk to you."

I roll my eyes. It's like I didn't even say anything. Sometimes, it's like Deacon and Kelsey are running things around here and I just write the checks.

"Yeah? And what are her qualifications?" I ask. Not because I'm troubleshooting her but because I'm actively curious. Kelsey has never invited anyone here. She's prickly at best around us and that means she's hard to get close to – for anyone.

"Well, she's cute, she seems only mildly insane, and she seems to need a place to work. Seeing how you don't exactly have the business school breaking down your door, I figured she'd be as good a shot as any."

I lean forward over the bar and pluck a cherry from the fruit tray. "What do you mean, only mildly crazy?"

Kelsey knocks back a shot of vodka straight up. Good god, the woman can drink. But I've never seen her drunk. Which, for working in a bar, is saying something.

"She was muttering something under her breath when she nearly ran into me. Someone in her life has clearly pissed her off."

I lift one eyebrow. "She doesn't have a Freddy Krueger starter kit or anything?"

"Not that I'm aware of." Kelsey hands off two pink drinks that are smoking on top. "Maybe some mild psychoses but nothing we haven't seen before."

Deacon shakes his head and passes her a couple of shot glasses. "We're used to our own special flavor of crazy around here. The kind that comes with a literal trigger warning."

Kelsey rolls her eyes and laughs. "These are the kinds of jokes that run off the high-paying clients. First rule of veteran crazy club: we don't talk about veteran crazy club."

It's Deacon's turn to roll his eyes. "That was pretty terrible."

She takes a bow.

And apparently, all is right in my little world once again.

CHAPTER 3

Parker

THE PINT ISN'T what I expected. Something loud and grinding is blasting from an ancient jukebox that actually has flipping discs to scroll through. The brick walls are accented with black and white photos and small flags of different colors. I'm sure they represent something but I'm not sure what.

Despite the dark interior, it feels homey, not cold or threatening. There are small candles at each table, nestled in glass jars and low-hanging lamps over a pool table near the jukebox.

I stand there for a moment, taking in how utterly stark the contrast is between this place and the Baywater where I usually hang out. Mostly because my father lets me run a tab there and doesn't complain because I rarely run it up too high.

But here, there's a different atmosphere altogether. Here there's no uptight piano music, no waiters in stiff white shirts that disappear as soon as they take your order.

Here is bar food and loud music. Laughter that's both too loud and comfortable all at the same time.

I am not at home here. It's too unrestrained. Too unsettled.

But I'll be damned if I chicken out now. I spot the girl from the quad behind the bar and make my way to her, dodging at least three eye-fuckings along the way.

Some things, sadly, are remarkably the same.

Her face lights as she spots me. "Hey, you made it. I honestly didn't think you'd show."

I smile at the welcome. "Really?"

She shrugs. "Figured the worst that could happen was you wouldn't show. If you did, you'd make my boss pretty damn happy because he's been in denial about looking for an intern for a while." She sticks out her hand. "I'm Kelsey, by the way."

"Parker."

Kelsey eyes me for a second. "I know why you're here," she says quietly. She holds up her finger, then starts pouring different liquids into a glass. A shake over one shoulder in the mixing glass and then a cherry on top and she slides it toward me. "Had a fight with the other half, didn't you?"

I grin and take a sip of the drink. "What's this called?"

"Breakup Sex."

I try not to choke. It's fruity with a bite of vodka behind it. "It's really good."

"I know. I was inspired the night I came up with it."

"Bad breakup?"

She lifts her own glass in mock salute. "Just one of many that I'd just as soon forget."

I sip the rest of my drink. "So did you find the financial aid office?"

"Yep. Now if only they knew how to access the GI Bill without requiring seventeen dead trees, I'd be okay."

I frown. "Does it really take that many?"

"Maybe only one tree. Or a sapling. Who knows? All I know is that nothing is easy these days."

"So you're a soldier?" Something about her mannerisms doesn't surprise me at all. "You're too pretty to be a soldier."

Kelsey shoots me a side eye that I'm pretty sure means I should drop dead. "There's this meme out there of stupid shit that civilians say to female soldiers." She winks at me and pours for the guy next to me who is trying not to look like he's staring down my shirt. "Google it sometime. Eyes up here, honey," she says to Peeping Tom.

I flinch, completely ignoring the guy next to me. "Sorry. I didn't mean to—"

"I know. That's why I'm still talking to you." There's no animosity in those words. Which surprises me. "The most difficult thing about being in this town is that every college student I encounter swears they know more about military life than me."

"I bet you hear all kinds of stupid things," I say. I'm suddenly remembering my class last semester. Where I was the know-it-all college student who knew more about life and violence than my classmate who'd been deployed.

I suddenly feel two inches tall.

"You know what's great about being in the Army?" Kelsey slides a glass of water toward me. She points at a few of the guys scattered around the bar. "Every one of these dudes doesn't know me from Adam. But I feel more at home around these men than I do with my own family." She points a straw at me. "That's powerful stuff right there."

I look down into my glass. I wouldn't know. But I don't say that. Because this is not the Poor Parker Party.

She taps the edge of my glass. "Hey. You know what solves all the world's problems?"

"Please don't say whiskey."

Kelsey laughs. "Well, I was going to say whiskey but since you took that off the list I'll say penis. Like really good, grinding sex to get out all the aggression and frustration, you know?"

"No, can't say that I do," I mumble. She is seriously talkative in a no boundaries kind of way. "I'm not really sure how I feel about you sharing your penis fetish. I mean, it's cool and all but this is only our first date."

Kelsey promptly laughs her ass off. "Oh my sweet Jesus. You've never been well and truly fucked, have you?"

"I'm quite sure I have no clue what you're talking about. And that sounds really painful, to be honest." I toss back a large gulp of my drink, needing something to wash down the flames on my face.

She hands me another drink. "Bottoms up, honey. Sex should never hurt. Unless you want it to. Then, like, game on and all that. Get spanked to your little heart's content."

I choke on my drink and valiantly try not to spew it across the bar. It burns a little as I try not to laugh. "That's a hell of a visual."

Why am I even having this conversation? "The last time I had to talk about sex was the morning after I lost my virginity. And I didn't exactly get good advice on how to make the burning stop."

"Burning? What the fuck? Is your other half like Lucifer or something? Or," she pauses. "He didn't give you a—"

"No! No. It just…wasn't very good. I wasn't really ready, that's all."

Kelsey leans closer. "Here's the thing. Sex is power. It's powerful. And we control that power. Men will do anything to get it." She lifts one eyebrow. "You should try it. There's nothing better than breakup sex. Someone new. Something to get you back in the game." She bites her bottom lip and nods. "Try it sometime."

I smile and shake my head. "I'm not that uninhibited."

She slides my second drink toward me. "Keep drinking and see where the night takes you." She winks at me once more. "I won't even introduce you to Eli until you're sober. That way you can make a good first impression and all that."

I drink because I can. Because tonight is about me and what I want.

And I want to stop hurting. To stop feeling trapped.

I want what Kelsey has. The easy smile. The confidence to control everyone at the bar with a flick of her hair or the flash of her eyes.

She's sharp.

She's free.

In ways that I will never be.

Eli

I STOP at the bottom of the stairs that lead up to my apartment over the bar. There's a small blonde standing there, staring at the Army photos lining the wall and holding a glass of something peach-colored and fizzy.

My first instinct is to dismiss her as just another rich girl in Durham for her Mrs. Degree.

There's an expression on her face that I can't read. Something quiet and laced with curiosity.

She's reading a small certificate I had framed years ago. After my first tour in First Cav, before I was shipped back east to the 82nd at Fort Bragg. But she wouldn't know that.

Her eyes are dark and laced with curiosity. "What's the Fiddler's Green?"

I pause next to her in the narrow hallway. There's no reason for her to be back here. The bathrooms are on the other side of the bar.

I'm not sure how I feel about her standing here, looking at the history that is meant for me and mine.

It's personal.

"It's where cavalrymen go when they die."

She looks up at me. "Cavalrymen?"

"The guys who used to ride horses in the Army but now drive around in tanks."

A small line knits between her brows. "Is everyone at this bar in the Army?"

I almost smile at the incredulity in her question. "Not currently. They tend to frown on facial hair. But once upon a time, yes."

A lifetime ago.

She looks like every other sorority girl in this damn town. Perfect golden hair, perfect lips in the perfect glossy pout, perfect body that's tight enough to make a blind man weep.

She's got "trouble" written on every curve attempting to break free of her clothing.

But there's something in her eyes that catches my attention. It's not curiosity, exactly. It's something more. Something…hungry and searching. At least a little bit.

I have a rule about fucking the customers, especially ones who look like her. She's got a rich daddy somewhere who's probably connected enough to make my life a living hell for touching his daughter.

Granted, it's a recent rule that started off as a lack of interest, but it's still a rule.

My bartenders can do what they want. They're grown-ass adults, and one of the perks of working at a bar is getting laid any time they want.

But lately…lately it's just not fun. A few weeks ago, I was sitting in the hospital as Caleb tried not to drop dead on us, and the futility of it all hit me like an Abrams tank. The Pint. The trying to build a space for us. It's stupid. I'm not a company commander anymore. The guys who hang out in my bar are not my soldiers.

And I need to stop acting like they are. My Army life is behind me, and it's not coming back.

The very thoughts feel blasphemous, like Gary Owen himself is going to reach out from the grave and rip my heart out of my chest.

I study Trouble for a moment, weighing whether to answer any more questions. "I don't like talking about my time in the Army," I admit quietly.

"Isn't that a little ironic?" She motions toward the wall lined with pictures.

"My life is a study in contradictions."

She lifts one brow, letting the silence hang for a long moment. "I took a class on violence this semester," she finally says. "I don't understand why anyone would sign up for the Army. Why you would sign up to go to war." She narrows her eyes at me, studying me quietly. "Why did you go? Why did you sign up?"

It's a bold question, I'll give her that. And thank god it's not "was it like *Call of Duty*", my personal favorite conversation ender. My cock is definitely interested in answering her question but maybe later. He's not really a fan of my new rule or guideline or whatever it is.

But my heart and my head have different ideas. Ones that start and end with *oh hell no*. She might be slumming in my bar tonight, but she's definitely not my type. And her questions about violence hit a little too close to home. Questions I'm not interested in entertaining from a complete stranger. "It's complicated," is all I say instead, opting to let the conversation slide into something less raw, something more carnal.

She shifts then to turn a little more toward me. I catch a glimpse of a shadow on her arm beneath the edge of her top.

I don't ask permission. I nudge the lace edge of her top higher, revealing what looks suspiciously like where fingers might rest if they were grabbing someone.

I brush my fingers over her skin and my fingers are dusted with concealer. Just a hint, careful not to cross any lines. "Where'd you get these?"

She's tried to hide the damage, but she's not doing a very good job. Or maybe she is, and I just can't miss these things.

I'm like a magnet for the walking fucking wounded.

I can't help myself, but I can't turn away when someone is hurting. It's been ingrained in my DNA since I was eighteen years old.

Even a complete stranger.

I'm going to regret this. Of that much I'm sure. But the question is already hanging in the air between us.

She shifts then, folding her arms over her chest, angling her bruised arm away. The movement has the effect of physically blocking me. I'd have to be a dead man to not react to that much perfection as the motion presses her breasts against the edge of her low-cut top.

I'm a little annoyed at how easily distracted my dick is these days.

"That's a long story," she says. Her voice is thick and low. Sultry. Perfect for a late-night rendezvous in a bar. "I'll tell you mine if you tell me yours?"

I shake my head. "Sorry. Some stories aren't meant for telling."

I'm not a eunuch, and I'm damn sure not a warrior monk, but it's been a long time since someone at my bar caught my attention.

Her eyes flicker with disappointment then drop down to my beard, then down my arms and slowly, slowly back up, her gaze licking my senses as much as if she were actually touching me. Slowly. I've been mentally undressed before, but there is something completely erotic in the way she's eye-fucking me.

And the more she watches me, the more I realize I am in just the right frame of mind to let her do what she wants.

Because tonight, I don't want to remember my rules or my fucking honor or my purpose for being here. I want to get lost in sensation and touch and hot gasps and tight, wet bodies. Forget the hurt, forget the loss, forget every dark nightmare and twisted daydream.

What better way to forget than to lose myself in mindless sex for an hour or two?

CHAPTER 4

Parker

I NEEDED to get out of my apartment and away from the creeping sadness that threatened to drown me if I stayed alone one more minute.

Tomorrow, I will find the owner of The Pint. Tomorrow I will figure out how to unfuck my life.

But right now, I'm standing in a closed-in space with a man who looks like a real-life rendition of Jason Momoa, and my panties are currently hosting their own episode of *Celebration* at the idea of standing just a little bit closer. I should be at the Baywater Country Club drinking top-shelf martinis and celebrating with Kylie and Bethany. But I can't see them tonight. For more than the obvious reasons.

I was planning on drinking myself stupid and forgetting everything about the last twenty-four hours in the human garbage fire that my life has become. It hurts and goddamn it, I'm tired of it hurting. I'm tired of being there for everyone else while I have to smile and look pretty.

Tonight? I thought I wanted the raw pulsing music and the bodies crushed together. I thought I wanted the contact. The distraction.

Don't make a fuss, Parker. Don't say anything to embarrass me, Parker.

What did you do to deserve it, Parker? Why didn't you just do what he asked? Why do you always have to argue?

Anger crawls up my spine and squeezes my throat once more.

For once in my fucking life, I want someone to look at me and see me. Not my father's car, or my not-allowed-to-be-ex-boyfriend's tailored suits.

I want someone to see *me*. All of me.

I don't know what I wanted when I left the apartment, but I think I may have just found it.

And the man standing next to me with the dark beard and dark eyes and terrifying tattoos seems like just the guy to take care of everything for a night.

Except that he might be a little too perceptive. I didn't plan on him seeing the bruises on my arm. Guess I need to rethink that career as a makeup artist if my graduate school plans don't work out.

He's still watching me, a dark intensity in his eyes. An intensity that feels like a brushstroke over my skin.

I wonder what it would feel like to wake up wrapped in those massive arms, to feel those hands run over my skin while I sleep. What it feels like to be really touched instead of just positioned to receive.

My eyes burn, and I blink rapidly. I didn't set out to solve anything tonight. I came out to escape. To try and find some release from the trapped air in my apartment.

Instead I think I've found a solution in search of a problem.

The solution is a big man. Rough, too. The kind of man I

would expect my father would call to lead the construction on a new project.

It's his hands, though, that capture my attention. Big and flat and broad. They're a working man's hands. Not polished. Not cupped in anger.

Just matter-of-fact hands. Hands that would be honest.

Hands that would feel like heaven on my skin.

I look up to find him watching me. I've never physically felt a look before this moment, this lazy caress of a man's gaze moving inch by inch over my skin.

I part my lips. Just enough that he notices. His nostrils flare.

"Careful, little girl." His voice is thick and deep and smooth. Like the gaze still trailing over my body.

"Or what?" I whisper. Kelsey's voice slides through my brain.

This is foolish. Utterly stupid.

This is power.

And it is exactly what I need tonight. I need to feel needed. Wanted.

Tonight isn't about rational thought. It's about the opposite. About going in blind, completely on instinct.

"I'm not sure you want to find out."

But he has not moved away. He hasn't turned his back on me, and he hasn't dismissed me as some childish twat playing grownup.

God, but those words burn in my ears.

"Maybe I do."

The muscles in his neck bunch beneath the thick beard. "Do you always hit on random men at bars?"

I press my lips together and dare to take a single step closer. "Nope. You'd be my first."

He lifts one brow. "Oh yeah? What's the occasion?" He jerks his chin toward me. "It doesn't have to do with the bruises, does it?"

I lift my glass to my lips. Slowly I part them, letting the ice cube bounce off the tip of my tongue. When I lower it, his eyes are locked on my mouth. "No," I whisper. "It's got nothing to do with them."

Nothing and everything. But he doesn't need to know that. He only needs to take me someplace and touch me.

Me. I need him to see *me*.

He moves in then with a quickness that catches me off guard. In an instant, he is right there, right in my space. I can smell the faint, smoky scent of him. Something woodsy and spicy and smoky.

It's all I can do to stay still. To not back down from the challenge he presents in that single breath of space.

"What do you want?" A murmured question that feels like a demand.

The single word I need is lodged in my throat. It's thick and heavy, filled with potential and promise.

"You," I finally say.

"Why?"

Such a complicated question. I search his face, looking for an answer, a lie, something simple to fill the space left by his question.

I lift my hand, afraid he'll see it tremble. It takes every ounce of willpower I've got to slide my fingers over his forearm. I'm surprised by the raw power beneath my touch. I expected the tattoos to be physical manifestations of the violence on his flesh.

His skin is hot and smooth. My hand looks pale and small against it.

"You seem..." I lift my eyes to his, never removing my hand. "You seem like a straightforward kind of guy."

A man with rough hands and dark ink carved into his skin. A man so unlike the men I'm used to, it's not even funny.

I lift my hand to his cheek, just above the edge of his beard. I've never touched a man with facial hair before.

He is still beneath my touch. A moment before I'm about to

press my palm to his cheek, he grips my wrist. Not hard enough to hurt, but he definitely gets my attention.

"Not here."

I swallow. My mouth is suddenly dry. "Where?"

He jerks his chin toward the dark hallway behind us.

I follow him silently, wishing he was already touching me, making me feel, letting me pretend I matter, even if it's only for a few minutes.

He leads me through the maze of small tables and patrons at various stages of intoxication. Away from the noise and the smell of fries and smoke and cologne and all the good things that bars have.

We step out of the noise and into shadows and silence. He doesn't pounce, doesn't push me against the wall and run those rough hands over my skin.

Instead, he leans against it—a casual, arrogant male.

Waiting.

I know for what.

For me to make the first move.

For me to step into the space between us. For me to touch him first.

I want to.

But I am paralyzed. Rooted to the damp concrete beneath my feet. The cool night air might as well be chains, holding me, restraining any thought or movement.

He doesn't move. His arms are folded over his broad, heavy chest, his t-shirt straining against his body.

The silence hangs on, stretching and thick and tight.

"Scared?" he finally whispers. A dare. A terrible, wicked promise in that single word.

"Should I be?" My throat is tight and dry.

His answer is nothing I expect.

And everything I want.

CHAPTER 5

Eli

I DON'T TAKE advantage of people. My tactical officer at West Point tried to make me into a leader who could squeeze the most out of his people with the minimum amount of effort.

I was supposed to get shit done. Not ask how it got that way.

And why in the fuck am I thinking about that forty-seven month experience at Castle Grayskull right now?

The woman in front of me…there's more to this story than a sorority sister out for a casual fuck. That might have been what I thought she was after back in the bar, but now, out in the open, I'm no longer certain.

She's not being coy or shy. There is genuine uncertainty in her eyes. As though she just realized she's stepped into a secluded alley with a dude twice her size, sporting a beard and enough ink to make her mother drag her back to church.

And damn it, I don't want this. I thought…I thought she would be a nice distraction from the memories tonight.

But it won't be what either of us want. Or need. I honestly think she might shatter if I touch her, and not in the good kind of way.

No matter how much she might try to pretend otherwise.

I push off the wall and step into her space. Slowly, giving her time to back away. I lift my hand again, making sure she sees it coming. Someone hurt her and the bruises are recent enough that it might have been earlier today, maybe last night.

A spike of violence hits my blood, causing my fingers to tremble. I release my breath through clenched teeth as I gently trace the edge of her tender flesh. "Whoever did this doesn't deserve you," I whisper.

I want my words to matter. I want them to sink in. I want her to walk away and be okay.

I know it is infinitely more complicated than that.

She closes her eyes as I slip my fingers down the smooth line of her throat. She trembles, a subtle movement I wouldn't have noticed had I not been completely engrossed in the moment.

In the simple act of touching her.

Her skin is soft, her pulse a scattered race beneath my fingertips. I cup her face. Gently, so gently. She presses against my palm, exposing her neck just a little.

The urge to press my lips to that pulse point pounds through me. I close my eyes, breathing deeply, reminding myself that I am not an animal. I will never again release the beast inside me.

I am...I am me. Not the shadows and pain. Not the war, etched into my skin.

I am not the callous bastard the Army tried to make me into.

Only when I am certain of my control do I lean closer and press my lips to her neck. She makes a warm, smooth sound, deep in her throat.

"It's soft."

I nuzzle her skin. "What is?" I whisper.

"Your beard. I didn't imagine it would be soft."

I smile at the amazement in her voice, nuzzling her neck. "What did you think it was going to feel like?"

She shifts and looks up at me. The shadows in her eyes are still there. No magical sex to clear away the pain.

Maybe that should be hell on my ego but it's not.

I'm too cynical about the cost of war to think it can be healed with a good cry and a bottle of Jack.

Her lips curl slightly at the edges. "I don't know. Scratchy?" Her palm comes to rest over my heart. "This isn't exactly what I had in mind," she whispers. She doesn't meet my gaze when those words cross her lips.

"I kind of figured that."

I lower my hands, leaving her in control, letting her set conditions here.

She narrows her eyes at me. "Any other red-blooded American male would have had me naked up against that wall in thirty seconds flat." She tips her head. "Why didn't you?"

There is uncertainty in that question. A painful kind. The kind that tells me about wounds that run deep. Very deep.

"Maybe I wanted to know your name first."

She shakes her head. "That's not what this was supposed to be."

It's a single sentence, the sharpest blade. Honest, even as it cuts me. She'll be perfectly happy to fuck me here in this alley but can't be bothered to ask me my name.

Something about the acknowledgment that she's using me for a cheap, anonymous fuck burns on a fundamental level.

"Why are you here tonight?" There is an edge to my voice.

Her eyes sweep down over the full sleeves of tattoos and back up to my beard before she meets my eyes. "Why are you asking questions?"

There's something deeply unsettling about this moment.

I step into her space now, unreasonably angry at what she's trying to do here. I back her up against the wall. "So tell me. Is it the tattoos, the beard, or the fact that I work in a bar that made you want to fuck me tonight? What points were you trying to score with your ex? Or is it your daddy?"

She flinches but doesn't look away. She holds my gaze for a long moment, maybe more. Then she finally looks away, into the darkness at the end of the alley. "Neither." It is a long time before she looks back at me. "I just wanted someone to touch me."

She ducks out beneath my arms and disappears. Into the darkness. Away from me.

And I am alone once more. Just like I will always be.

Parker

IT WOULD HAVE BEEN SIMPLER for me to go back into the bar and get hammered with Kelsey but I have some pride. I honestly can't face the burning embarrassment of my failed attempt to be something more than a doll playing dress up. It would be awkward as hell but if I got drunk, I wouldn't care about the shame of rejection, right?

Except that I can see him looking at me with the same level of disgust I see in the mirror and, well, I get enough of that on a daily basis.

My apartment isn't far from The Pint and honestly, it's better if I go home. I can drink alone and no one else will get hurt. At least not tonight, anyway.

I guess nobody gets what they want these days.

I am running away again. Something I've never been particularly good at.

I was trying to get away from the silence. I want it to stop. I don't want to hear the sound of my voice. I don't want to relive the shame or the hurt or any of it.

For just one night, I wanted to be a regular girl having a regular hookup at a regular bar.

But there was nothing normal about tonight. Not the way he looked at me. Not the way he touched me.

My apartment is silent and cold.

I crawl into bed. I can still feel his lips on my throat, the touch of his beard against my skin. It was soft; his lips warm and moist where they traced over my flesh.

And then he stopped. Just as quickly as he started, everything came to a screeching halt.

And he knew. He fucking knew I was not there to feel good, not there for me, but to lash out. I don't know how he knew, how he saw it, but he did.

He was actually pissed about it. I could have walked up to any other guy in that bar and asked them to take me outside and fuck me and they would have. I don't say that to brag, but I understand how men work. They are wired to their cocks.

So why didn't he?

The street lamps cast long pale strips of light across my bed. I lie there, wondering about him. What is his name? He has so many tattoos. I've never seen a man with so much body art. I suddenly very much want to know if the tattoos extend across his chest, his back.

Why couldn't he have kept kissing me? His touch made me feel desirable. Like a real person, not the shadow of who I am supposed to be.

He could have backed me against the wall. It would have hurt. Brick does not feel good against skin. I wish I didn't know that, but I do.

He could have lifted my skirt with those big, rough hands. God, but it would have felt amazing. The bite of pain mixed with the pleasure of his touch.

I squeeze my thighs together. My hand drifts down my belly. I know what I'll find. I know what pleasure can and cannot happen between my thighs.

Davis has made it abundantly clear that I'm inadequate in all the important ways. There's really no coming back from that in a relationship. Not that there was ever really a relationship there to begin with.

I have some pride, after all.

But *him*—that's how I think of the man at the bar—his touch would have been good. He would have known to slide his finger over me until I was wet. He would have waited until I was ready instead of pounding into me and telling me I don't love him because I'm not wet enough.

It would still have hurt with him. It might not have come even remotely close to the fantasy that is making me arch my back and spread my thighs.

In my head, he is standing there, watching me, urging me on. Stroking my thighs with his big, rough hands. Whispering encouragement.

Whispering my name.

Covering my hand with his. Slowly drawing our index fingers through the slick, wet heat that doesn't exist in my reality. Slowly drawing the pleasure from the pain.

Slowly, slowly filling me.

Showing me that it doesn't have to hurt. That it doesn't have to be like it always has been.

That there is someone out there who will see me for me. Who will not be drawn in by my father's money or the power my name evokes.

Someone who will stroke me with his fingers as I come and whisper my name and hold me as I shatter.

Tomorrow. Tomorrow, I will start to take back my life.

Always tomorrow.

Because the pain of today hurts too much.

CHAPTER 6

Eli

As MUCH AS my cock is highly pissed at me, fucking that woman would have been the wrong thing to do. My dick isn't speaking to me right now because of my moral standing on these types of situations. Morals don't get a guy laid.

I've made plenty of the wrong choices in my life. I don't need to add to my list of regrets.

So why the hell am I still thinking about her? Especially when I've been up for six hours and have already had three cups of coffee and two meetings with distributors. I should be thinking about work, not how her skin tasted.

Christ, why didn't I take her up on the offer? She was so fucking primed it wasn't even funny. She'd melted the minute I touched her and I hadn't even really got started. One touch of my lips on her throat and she'd practically started purring.

My life has gotten too damn serious these days. For a guy who runs a bar, I'm depressingly celibate.

Thirteen hours later and I'm still wired for sound after that stunt in the alley. I've got nothing to do with the pent-up need throbbing in my balls. Which means I'm strung out from too much coffee and not nearly enough sex.

Maybe I should take an hour before I head into the bar. Detour upstairs to my apartment over the bar and spend some private time with a bottle of lotion and some creative and filthy thoughts.

Jesus, I'm like a twelve-year-old with a walking hard-on and no self-control.

To spite myself, I'm not going upstairs. I'm going to be an adult.

I arrive at my building—irritated from fighting traffic on I-40 —in time to find someone has parked their fucking Mercedes in my parking spot.

I sit there for a minute, staring at the sleek silver car that's sitting in the parking spot that I pay five hundred dollars a month to reserve.

I don't have time to be riding around looking for a place to park. Not as a resident or as a business owner.

Ignoring how much of a tool it makes me feel like, I block them in. Someone will get the message soon enough. Hell, I pay the city enough damn money for that spot. And it's meant specifically for days like this when I can't afford to be running around looking for somewhere to fucking park.

Which makes me really fucking cranky as I walk into the bar. Deacon is already there, bright-eyed and far too bushy-tailed, cleaning the chalkboard behind the bar and prepping it for the day's drink specials.

Deacon has more ink—and more scar tissue—than I will ever have but he's magic behind the bar.

"The Pale Horse Brewery was already here," he says by way of greeting. "I took the delivery and left the paperwork on your desk."

I clap him on the shoulder as I lean down and pull an iced

coffee from the micro fridge beneath the bar. Because more coffee is exactly what I need right now. I'm lucky I'm not pissing pure caffeine at this point. "You are clearly on your way to sainthood."

I count myself lucky every single day that I was able to lure Deacon away from the big money he was making up in New York City. I still don't honestly know what made him make the change. He said he was ready to leave the city behind. I don't think that's the entire story, but I learned a long time ago that when guys are ready to talk, they'll talk.

And he may never be ready.

But I'll be here if he ever is.

I don't ask, though. I'd hate for him to get buyer's remorse and go back to the big city he's left behind to come work for me.

I head into the office and start tallying receipts. I already dropped the deposit at the bank, since it's like asking to get robbed to keep anything over fifty bucks on the premises. Durham is a weird town undergoing rapid gentrification. On this block there are houses going for a quarter of a million dollars; two blocks over, you still have rabid poverty.

There's a distant shout from the bar area. I usually don't get involved in those unless I have to—my bartenders can generally handle themselves.

But the noise is coming closer.

"Who the hell blocked me in?"

I frown at the angry female voice. It's not a voice that's attached to any of the women I have working for me.

"My boss." Deacon sounds perfectly reasonable. Ms. Mercedes, however, sounds just this side of irate, hissing kitten. "You're in his spot."

And then said kitten is standing in my office.

I lean back in my chair, folding my arms over my chest. The universe is fucking with me. I must have kicked a puppy in a previous life. Or at least stepped on a snail. Christ, I don't need this right now.

Of-fucking-course it's the woman from last night. Because my life is a goddamned cliché.

She's wearing white designer jeans that are damn near painted on her tight ass. To be honest, I give myself high marks for not staring at those exquisite curves, the curves that just last night filled my hands.

Yeah, I'm working toward my own canonization. It's a herculean effort to drag my eyes off her body and focus on the irritation looking back at me.

Because that's helping get my one-track mind out of the gutter.

Everything about her screams Old Money, from the expensive wedge espadrilles to the fine stitching on the pale peasant blouse that does nothing to disguise her perfect body.

She looks like she belongs on a yacht in Bar Harbor, not slumming in my bar in downtown Durham.

And yet here she is.

I'm not prepared for the force of my own reaction. My cock doesn't normally have a mind of his own, but he's damn sure stood up and taken notice now that she's stormed into my office, her heels clicking on the polished concrete floor.

I'm definitely not into rich girls. I got that out of my system last year when I discovered just how high maintenance they could be.

Which means I'm being a dick. Still.

It smarts that last night I was only good enough for her to fuck to piss off Daddy or whoever.

I finally break the silence. "Is there a problem?"

She's going to have to make the first move. I might be highly pissed off right now, but if she'd rather pretend that last night didn't happen, I'm fine with that.

It's no sweat off my sac if she sets the pace. It's powerful, letting a woman have control.

I bet she doesn't even know how to let go. She's probably

always in charge of everything. That's the way money works. Always has.

"Yeah, you've blocked me in."

"I think Deacon already told you. You're in my spot."

She rotates her jaw in a way that reminds me of my younger sister when she's in her most pissy mood. "And you blocking me in gets you your spot back how?"

I fight the urge to smirk at her. She's pissed off enough. "It doesn't. But it does make you—or whoever—have to come in and ask me to move. At which time I can point out that I pay the city of Durham a very pretty penny for this private parking space for my employees."

"Your employees?" There is a level of disdain in her voice that I haven't heard since I told my father and stepmother I wasn't a virgin and—oh, the humanity—had gotten my first tattoo when I'd come back from Iraq the first time.

I lift one eyebrow. "Yes, my employees."

"You're...the owner?" Angry Kitten Parking Space Stealer has consumed my attention from the moment she walked into the office, so I notice when all the color flushes from her face. It could be comical if she weren't so seriously pissed about the car.

"You could try sounding a little less shocked, honey."

"Sorry." She clears her throat and sniffs, then shifts her stance. It's an almost physical change in her. "But I was here for a meeting with the owner of The Pint."

"Which is why you parked in his spot?" I ask. Yes, it's weird that I'm talking about myself in the third person, but she's got me all twisted up right now. I'm lucky I'm even able to form a conscious thought.

She finally flushes, and it is fucking adorable. "So...yeah... could we possibly move beyond the parking spot?"

I lean forward, bracing my elbows on my desk. I'm enjoying myself tremendously for no apparent reason. And my dick clearly has an opinion about how we feel about that. I haven't had a

Thayer Dragon in a long, long time but I'm about to embarrass myself like a nineteen-year-old cadet getting called to the boards.

Which means I'm not getting my happy ass out of this chair for anything short of a nuclear apocalypse.

But I can still enjoy this moment. "Maybe if you say sorry."

"It's just a parking space." She sighs and folds her arms over her chest, mirroring my stance. And quite literally digs in her heels. "Fine. Is this about last night?"

Parker

I DID NOT MEAN to bring that up. I honestly was hoping to forget the whole damn incident. But oh no, I have a pathological inability to keep my mouth shut.

And seeing him sitting there, looking smug and sexy and quite possibly undressing me with his eyes, I'm pretty sure there's no way out of this situation while still retaining my panties.

And I'm okay with that. After last night, I'm pretty sure they've disintegrated just by being in the same room as him.

If only my reality was as erotic as my imagination.

This whole situation just went sideways. Because now, instead of a brief moment of insanity against a cold, damp brick wall, I've now got to choke down a giant helping of crow and ask him for a job.

Jesus, you can't make this shit up.

"What *about* last night?" he asks mildly.

I'm reasonably certain his lips are quirked at the edges. And sweet baby Jesus his mouth is ridiculously full beneath that beard.

I never thought beards were sexy before but in this moment, I'm ready to head to the great North Woods and molest an LL Bean catalog.

"Well, ah..." Oh god this is awkward. It's one of those moments when you hope the earth will open up and swallow you whole. 'Course that never happens, so I guess I need to start digging my way out of the massive cavern I've managed to dig into because I decided to try something new that backfired in an epic and unforgettable way.

Guess there's only one way through this massive wall of man who is determined to make me squirm and not in any way that I'd like to be squirming.

"Thank you."

Both of those dark brows shoot up, then down into a scowl. His lips are parted, just a little, pulled into a thoughtful line. "For what? Not sexually assaulting you?"

Holy crap he's not making this easy. "I was perfectly willing to participate in whatever might have happened in that alley last night."

"Okay. Then what are you thanking me for, if that's what you wanted and that's not what you got?"

I close my eyes and take a deep breath. I can feel him waiting, like a feral cat stalking its prey. *Patient, oh so patient.*

I shift my purse to my other shoulder. My sleeve shifts with it and his eyes are drawn to something I'd rather forget.

"Those don't look any better in the full light of day." His voice is soft. There is an edge to his voice now, a latent energy that hadn't been there a moment before.

"Yeah, well, I suck at makeup." Bad attempt at a joke. He doesn't even crack a half-smile.

He scrubs his hand over his mouth and makes a noise deep in his chest. "Are you safe? Are you away from whoever did this?"

The simplicity of that question strikes me, hard, in the chest. My lungs tighten and I suddenly can't take a full breath.

All because he just asked a question that was one hundred percent about me, just me.

And he doesn't even know me.

"I am." A statement that is mostly true. "Look, last night I was hurting. And I wanted you to…distract me from that hurt. I'm not sure I wouldn't have woken up with a fist full of regrets this morning. So thank you. For being one of the good ones."

"I'm no saint," he says quietly. Again—simple words laced with layers of meaning. There is so much more to this man than the beard and the tattoos.

"I don't think you are. But every single guy I know would have fucked me six ways from Sunday last night and left me with the regrets." I breathe out hard, because this is a terrible conversation to have when you're sober. It would be so much better if I were having this conversation with one of Kelsey's drinks in hand. What did she call them? Breakup Sex. And just like that, I'm thinking about the man sitting at his desk, looking like a pagan god playing at businessman, doing terrible things to my body.

I clear my throat, wishing the images away. Or, at least, tucked away where I can enjoy them later.

"But you didn't. So, thank you."

He surprises me then. In a single move, he is around the desk. I don't remember him being this tall, this overwhelming last night. His shoulders block out the light, the solid wall of his chest consuming everything I can see.

He smells the same, though. Something smoky and warm that makes me want to bury my face in his neck and breathe him in.

He is utterly gentle when he reaches up, cupping my cheek softly. His thumb rasps over my cheek. "There are plenty of things in this life to regret. Sex should never be one of those things," he murmurs.

He doesn't move for a long moment. I don't think I want him to. I want to stay right there, forever, and draw on his strength. Use it to hold myself upright. To gather my strength to face the world.

I'd touched myself last night, imagining his fingers, his mouth.

But I never thought to put a name to that touch.

What does that say about me and the life I've lived up until now?

I swallow. "I'm Parker."

He takes a step back then, leaning on his desk, his forearms corded and braced against the edge. "Eli."

I resent the space between us. The ease with which he backs away and acts like the world didn't just tip beneath his feet. "So what did you need to see me about?"

"I'm here about the internship."

He arches one dark brow and the move is nothing but pure male arrogance. "The Mercedes in my parking spot does not suggest starving college student." And just like that, we are back to where we started. He folds his arms over his chest, and I cannot miss the way the corded tendons press against his skin.

"Yeah, well, the Mercedes in your parking spot doesn't buy me a passing grade for my honors project or help me with my application for the executive management program at the business school."

He frowns. "I didn't post an internship ad."

I pull out the flyer from my purse. He mumbles something that sounds suspiciously like "Deacon", but I can't be sure. I wonder if that's Mr. Attitude out front.

But I'm more concerned about Mr. Tattoo and Beard standing in front of me. Heat radiates from his body, drawing me closer, like a dying woman craving just one taste of salvation.

Eli. His name is Eli.

"You're going to have to work a little harder than that to convince me why you're here instead of asking Daddy for help. Doesn't he have the right connections to get you a job at a consulting firm or something?"

I run my tongue over my top lip at the disdain dripping from his words. "Pretty judgmental to make all these assumptions about me, isn't it?"

"Am I wrong?"

Heat flashes across my skin. Damn it. It's everything I can do not to stomp my foot and start making demands.

"Not exactly," I finally admit. I push out a hard breath. "Look, I don't want to ask my dad to get one of his friends to help me with this project."

"Which doesn't tell me why you're here and not somewhere else more suitable."

"Maybe I want to learn how the bar business works. There's tremendous growth opportunity in this market segment. I specialized in marketing. I could really use the stuff I've learned to help you work your branding and market placement."

He frowns, and I can't help but miss the slight downturn of his lips at the edge of his beard. "It's actually incredibly crowded."

"Not the way you're doing it. Who the hell thinks up a place that does pancakes and beer?"

"Anyone who has ever been out drinking at three a.m. and decided they needed pancakes but they weren't ready to call it a night yet." He is scowling at me. "Besides, that was a failed experiment. No one who actually runs a bar wants to pull the graveyard shift and be part of the pancake crowd at four in the morning."

I should probably be at least a little nervous. Or maybe feel a hint of embarrassment. But he hasn't asked me to leave yet, so that's a good thing, right?

"Why are you really here?"

Damn it, why did I have to pick the one guy who can see right through me? "I told you already." But the words feel dishonest at best. Nothing in my life is that simple.

He steps into my space again. "You're not a very good liar."

"Actually, I am usually much better at this sort of thing."

"What, lying?" There goes that dark brow again, rising into the air with an arrogance that's starting to get annoying.

"Negotiating." I shift my purse, suddenly highly conscious about how everything I am wearing—from my top to my purse to my shoes—screams that I am out of my environment.

"So let me get this straight. Last night, you came here for a revenge fuck to piss off Daddy or the ex or whoever. Today, you're here looking for a job when you could pick up the phone and ask Daddy for help with this." He's still studying me, still standing far too close. "I don't want anything to do with you and your daddy issues, honey. They have counselors for that kind of shit."

There is hurt in those words. It's subtle but there, blazing for the world to see if only it would look closely enough. I'm not sure I dare to step this close to the fire. But I can't leave, either. Because leaving would be a retreat. It would make me a coward. "I know this looks bad but I'm asking for a chance."

"Why should I hire you?" He straightens, consuming the space in front of me again. "What can you possibly bring to this assignment other than being a pain in my ass?"

CHAPTER 7

Eli

SHE'S SLUMMING. It's been written in red in everything she's done from the minute she set foot in my bar last night.

And I am perfectly aware that girls like her do exactly this kind of thing before they settle down into their Ralph Lauren photoshoot kind of life. The kind of life where the whole family gets dressed in white button-down shirts and sits on the beach at sunset. She isn't the first girl who's come into my bar looking for a wild time, and she won't be the last.

But she is the first one to make me feel all twisted up and…just twisted up. There's nothing else. Just dark arousal and deep, abiding curiosity about why she's really standing here. Who put the bruises on her. And why the fuck I give enough of a shit to want to know more.

This girl, though. There's something about the way she moves through the world that reminds me of where I came from—and where I steadily avoid returning to. At the same time, there's something about her that pulls at me just as if she were one of the guys I've managed to round up. It's not just the bruises on her arm, either. Those are surprisingly common around here, too.

Funny how people think the only folks who get abused are poor women.

She doesn't answer my question for an impossible length of time. She shifts her weight from side to side, biting her lip as she searches for an answer. Finally, she takes a subtle, deep breath. "Last night I asked you why you joined the Army. Why you signed up to go to war." She hesitates, trying hard not to look like she's hesitating.

"One of the things we can't explain in economics is why people make decisions that aren't in their best interests. Why people work hard when there's no financial incentive. Why people volunteer for war. Your bar is like that. This place charges premium prices in a crowded niche of businesses that all charge premium prices, and yet you're standing out in the local economy." She pauses. "I want to know why."

"And this is why you won't ask your father for help?"

"I love how you keep assuming my father is wealthy and has all the right connections. What if it's my mom?"

"Is it?"

She shoots me a dirty look. "No," she grumbles. And it's fucking cute. Jesus, I need to get laid. She shifts again.

"What if I'm not hiring?"

It's completely irrational. I've built this business with my own two hands. I'm proud as hell of it and what it means to all of us who work here. There's no logical reason for me not to hire her. And yet, I'm resisting.

"Okay, but if you start taking on interns from the business school it'll get you tied into the institution and could potentially create some lucrative catering opportunities, among other things."

I lift one eyebrow. "How did you know I wanted to expand into catering?"

"I did some homework this morning. The write up in the local paper on your bar last summer is one example. It's a case study on how your business model doesn't fit into the right mold but is still doing exceedingly well when it shouldn't be. And now that you've expanded into whiskey, you're poised to really break out. It's a perfect complement to your existing niche, but you need to exploit it and figure out how to make room for higher-end clients among your current clients who are more grounded in daily life."

She's sharp, I'll give her that; and she knows what she's talking about. I move back around my desk, primarily to put some space between us before I do anything stupid. Again.

Everything is in its place. I'm hyper-organized—it's a sickness burned into my brain from my time at West Point. It didn't do anything to help me as a commander, though. No, I screwed that up big time.

"You really want to work here?"

She hasn't moved. She didn't move when I crowded into her space and she's not moving now. It's odd how I'm so used to movement and her stillness is both unsettling and grounding.

Every one of my employees is a veteran of some flavor or another. I've done that deliberately. It means there's a whole slew of underlying assumptions about how we work together that doesn't require extensive training or orientation.

Bringing her on is going to change the dynamics here.

But there is something about her that says she's one of us. There's no way a girl like her has been through the war, but she's been through something more serious than the perfect life that she's presenting to the world suggests.

"I really do."

I say nothing. Then after a moment, I nod.

"I need you to fill out employment paperwork," I finally say. I pull out the state forms from a drawer and hand them to her.

This girl is complicated. Very much so. And I don't need any more complications in my life. But as usual, common sense doesn't really apply when it comes to me gathering more people for my little island of misfit toys. There is something about her that calls to me.

If my dick could whimper, it would. By bringing her on board as my employee, it makes her one hundred percent off-limits. Which is good.

She extends her hand toward me, her face lighting up in a brilliant smile. "Thank you. I won't disappoint you."

Electricity snaps between us as I take her hand. Small and slender, she's clearly never lifted a shovel or fired a weapon in her life. She's not weak, though. Her grip is strong and solid, if small.

She looks down at our hands. For a moment, she is stiff, then she relaxes, her fingers curling around the base of my palm. It's a subtle shift but it's there.

And just like that, the tension eases away from her.

"This isn't the country club," I tell her. "There are fights here."

She tucks the paperwork into her oversized purse. "You've clearly not spent time at the Baywater. You should see how peckish old Southern women get over their favorite bar stool. Just last week, I saw a vicious slap fight between a Martha Stewart wannabe and Paula Dean's anorexic twin before the bartenders escorted them both to opposite sides of the bar."

Her response is not what I expected. I lean against my desk, feeling off-kilter yet oddly at ease, now that she's loosened up a little. "That is a seriously fucked-up visual."

"I've got a million of them." She pauses, then gives me a look that I can't read. "So can you move your car?"

Parker

I'VE NEVER FELT self-conscious about my car before. But as Eli moves his truck, I am suddenly and painfully aware of how different my life is from his.

He is standing in my rearview mirror as I pull away. He's a mystery that has only gotten more complicated in the last twenty-four hours.

I drum my fingers on the leather of my steering wheel as I head toward my apartment, my mind spinning over the abrupt shift in my life since meeting Eli.

My dash lights up as my phone rings.

Davis has a lot of nerve to call me. It's the third time he's tried calling me since yesterday.

Yeah, picking up his call is not going to happen. I need some space from him and all of his anxiety and stress. I don't want or need to be a doormat. My father isn't here to pressure me to be more supportive to Davis so I press "ignore" on my steering wheel—only for the dash to light up again, this time with my father's name.

Speak of the Devil and all that.

Once upon a time, I would have lit up to see his number on my phone. But he never calls to check on me. It's always about Davis.

But I'm still that pathetic little girl who needs Daddy's affection any way I can get it, so I answer the phone, knowing what his first words will be and knowing how much they will hurt, and doing it anyway.

"Hi, Daddy."

"What happened with Davis? Why aren't you taking his calls?"

Tap, tap tap. My nails drum a soothing rhythm into the leather and I suck in a deep breath, holding it for a long moment like I've learned to do in yoga. Trying to find the calm inside the storm of my emotions. "We're disagreeing about what to do this summer."

He sighs audibly. "It's that bad that you won't talk to him?" My father might as well have just mentioned the weather for all the emotion he puts into that sentence.

For a moment, I'm surprised at how much it doesn't hurt that he doesn't even say hi to me. I frown, unable to figure out where that hurt went.

Later. I'll unpack that later. Right now, I have to navigate this phone call.

"I'm working on getting over it. I'll call him. Later." After a whole lot of therapeutic drinking.

But I don't tell my father that.

I swallow the lump in my throat. I'm lying to my father. It doesn't feel good. But it's not crushing the air from my lungs like it normally does.

"I wish you wouldn't argue as much as you do. Davis is a good man."

I press my lips together and say nothing. Because clearly there is nothing I can say that will penetrate my father's views on the world and my place in it. I am a means to a son for him. Little more.

I wasn't always cynical about my relationship with Davis. Except that now, he feels less like a fiancé and more like a way to keep my relationship with my dad.

I haven't figured out a way out of that dilemma yet, which is why I'm having this conversation with my father instead of ignoring him.

I can practically hear the disappointment in his voice. "You're just having pre-wedding jitters. The engagement has already been posted in the society section of the *New York Times*. I'm sure you'll figure it out."

That is the most optimistic thing he can say right now.

I pull into my numbered parking spot in the parking garage and disconnect my phone from my car's Bluetooth. "I really have to go."

"Call Davis. Get things sorted out. He really loves you."

Our definitions of love have dramatically diverged since my mom died. Instead I make a noise in my throat and mumble something polite just to get off the phone, waiting for the familiar hurt that doesn't come.

I climb the stairs into my apartment and sink into my couch. My letter of intent for grad school is open on my computer. It's got all the relevant letterhead information but it's otherwise blank. I can't really come up with a reason why I want to go into the executive management program, other than that my dad wants me to get my MBA. It will help me be a good partner for Davis, helping me organize his personal affairs so he can focus on being a congressman.

Except that the longer my engagement with Davis goes on, the less it feels…right. It did, once upon a time. Was that only last summer when we started dating? It's hard to believe things have changed that much.

I haven't told anyone about how things have changed. I just smile and make polite noises when my friends gush over how lucky I am that Davis picked me. Like I'm a prize pony or something.

I take out my MacBook and start typing notes about my conversation with Eli. The terms of the agreement. The nuts and bolts of what he said, what I did. I don't know how much of this will end up in my final statement of purpose for the executive program but it can't hurt to jot things down.

My phone vibrates in my purse.

Your first shift is tonight at six.

I give in to my mischievous impulse.

This isn't exactly good employee communications. You should at least attempt to make employees feel as though they have a choice by asking instead of demanding. Or saying please once in a while.

The little bubbles appear as he types a response, then fade again. Then they're back.

Finally, a single word appears on my screen.

Please.

I grin, anticipation sliding through me.

I'll be there.
With fucking bells on.

CHAPTER 8

Parker

I'M STUCK. I've never actually had this problem before. I should have paid better attention when I was at the bar arguing with Eli for a job.

But I was too wrapped up in the bruises on my pride to pay attention.

I'm standing in my closet, and I have no idea what to wear.

I close my eyes, trying to remember if any of the waiters or waitresses were there when I'd met with Eli. Kelsey had been wearing a light-colored tank top with The Pint's logo the night before. What was everyone else wearing?

I can remember what Eli had on, though. Black t-shirt that hugged tight across his chest. If I close my eyes, I can still feel the heat from his body as he pressed against me. I squeeze my thighs together, needing to focus on my future first night at work.

Instead, my mind takes a fun little sexy detour that is not at all helpful with my current dilemma of what to wear.

Instead of focusing on clothing, all I can feel is the touch of his fingertips on my cheek. The soft scrape of his beard against my skin. The smoky taste of whiskey on his breath as his tongue slides against mine.

I've been kissed before but never like that. Like he has nothing but time to explore every aspect of my mouth. My body.

It really makes me wonder if he'd be as attentive in bed as he was with his mouth.

Except that he'd said no. What guy says no to no-strings attached sex? Aren't all guys supposed to be wild horn dogs only thinking about getting laid?

And just like that, the fantasy is over.

I drag my hands through my hair and focus on the task at hand. Eli seems like a pretty laid-back guy, dressing in jeans and t-shirts. So I assume if I show up dressed in something similar, it should be fine.

I shimmy into my favorite pair of skinny jeans and comfortable flats, then pull a fitted black v-neck t-shirt over my head. Sliding my hands over my sides and down my hips, I feel like I'm ready to face whatever the night has to offer.

I roll my eyes and finish straightening my hair. I don't want to look like I'm trying too hard, and at the same time, I don't want to stand out, either.

I change my bra.

I'm not stupid—I'm going to work in a bar, and if I want to make any tips I've got to play up my assets. Not that I need the money. I don't. But it's the principle of the thing—I can't not make good tips. It's a point of pride more than anything.

I think I'm finally ready to head to The Pint. I pause and take in my reflection. I look good.

I look like me again. For the first time since things with Davis started feeling off, I *feel* a glimmer of the real me looking back at me. Before the doubt. Before the whispers that I wasn't good enough started to consume my thoughts.

I want to capture the feeling, to hold it in my hands and use it to ward off the loneliness that stalks my nights. It's like a fleeting glimpse of light within the surrounding darkness.

But I can only avoid Davis for so long. Sooner or later, he's going to get frustrated with me and come back here if I ignore him for too long.

I wish I were brave enough to stand up to him. Tell him I took a class on feminist theory and I'm refusing to support the patriarchal hegemony of male dominance. Just thinking about his reaction makes me smile.

He'd explode.

Feminism doesn't exist for girls like me. Girls like me do what our fathers tell us to do. We smile when we're told to smile. We don't think. We don't argue.

And we definitely don't get to go slumming when we're supposed to be getting married to a congressman who's a rising star.

I suppose I'll get this out of my system then return to my regularly scheduled program of my perfectly scripted life.

God but that's depressing if I really think about it.

I can't. I have to push those thoughts aside.

Because I don't want to hear the disappointment in my father's voice that I'm overreacting. That I should be more accommodating to Davis's needs. That I should be grateful he picked me as his future wife.

Getting a job at Eli's is a small act of defiance that will end soon enough.

But I need this. I need this last taste of freedom.

I leave my phone and grab my keys and my purse.

I'm finally ready to live.

Even if it's only for a little while longer.

Eli

DEACON WALKS behind the bar where I'm updating the register software on the iPad I use to track sales. "So where do you want Sorority Barbie tonight?"

Deacon is grinning like he's incredibly proud of that nickname.

"You come up with that one all by yourself?"

His expression changes but he still grins. "It was the first thing I thought of when I met her. She's polished and perfect. Hopefully, she's got more under her pretty hair than an actual Barbie does."

"She might surprise you."

"I'm just hoping she's not a pain in the ass to train."

I lean back and fold my arms over my chest, leaving the iPad to download. "Is it Parker in particular you have a problem with or something more general?"

He pulls out the lemons and starts chopping them with a little too much emphasis tonight. "I don't trust her. The kind of people she comes from could cause problems for you here."

For a second, maybe more, my heart stops. There's no way he knows. He couldn't.

Deacon wasn't on that deployment. I've lost touch with most folks. I barely keep up with any of my classmates from West Point anymore.

Still. I have a healthy dose of paranoia that someday, my time in the Army will catch up with me. There have been high-profile articles written about my bar in national news outlets, and no one has put the pieces together yet. Maybe I'm safe.

It's not like I'm hiding it. Hell, I wouldn't be very smart if I was trying to hide things by running a bar where all the local vets seem to congregate, now would I?

I suck in a hard breath and hold it until my lungs burn, then release it. "I don't see how."

He lifts one brow and leans against the doorframe. "Her father is Bennington Hauser. He's a big wig at one of the largest defense contractors in D.C."

"How do you know this?" I hesitate. That is news. And it's also completely irrelevant.

He shrugs. "Google is your friend."

I'm not sure how I feel about his blossoming cyberstalking skills but I table it for now. It's not a crime to look up future employees. In fact, it's probably smart. Something I should do.

But I don't want to. Glass houses and all that, right? "So you think Daddy is going to come down here and pull rank?"

Deacon looks at me like I've started masturbating in public. "I'm just pointing out that the rest of us have our own complications but she's got complications that come with money. And with money comes power. So just be careful with her."

I nod, needing to put this to bed. "Tracking. Thanks for the warning."

My response is clearly insufficient as Deacon continues to violently slice the lemons. "You're the boss so when the shit starts pegging the fan, don't say I didn't warn you."

"And that, ladies and gentlemen, is an image I did not need."

Deacon makes a noise and just like that, we are back on even footing. "My job here is done." He glances down at his watch. "Kelsey hasn't shown up yet, either."

"Anyone check on her?"

"I texted her a couple of times but she's not responding. Don't forget she left with that Fifty Shades wannabe last night."

I rub my hand over my beard. "Sadly, I know exactly who you're talking about. Think she's okay?"

He lifts one shoulder. "She's an adult. She's more than capable of having carefree consensual sex without any of us commenting on who or what she does on her off-duty time."

He's being deliberately nonchalant. It's more than a little obvious. "Careful, or I'll send you to her place to make sure she's okay."

He makes a sound of disgruntled disbelief. Part of me wants to send him to check on her. Just to be on the safe side.

"Anyway, where do you want Sorority Barbie tonight? Register? Floor?"

"How about you use her name, for starters." I can see the leading edge of one of his moods coming on. "I think register is good for Parker's first night. It's Saturday so we're probably going to be slammed. It'll get her feet wet without pissing off the customers."

Deacon nods and slides the lemons into a tray, then wipes the knife and heads into the basement for more supplies. His warning hangs in the air long after he's gone. The iPad is still downloading, leaving me with little else to occupy my hands or my thoughts.

The war hasn't followed me home yet. I've made choices, surrounded myself with good people. I've tried to live a normal life, not one soaked in alcohol or regret. Deacon isn't wrong, though. Anything could resurrect that memory.

But that's not why he's pushing me on Parker. And that's not why I hired her. And it's definitely not the worry of a commander for one of his soldiers that is drawing me to Parker. No, it's something else. Something darker. Something infinitely more possessive. Something I haven't felt since…I can't remember when.

I really need to let Deacon run interference with her. Because I need to stay away. All the want in the world can't fix what ails me and no woman in the world would put up with my bullshit for more than a single night.

I finish up the iPad software and head back to my office to make sure it's synced on the WiFi network.

And damn near run over the one person I really should be avoiding.

CHAPTER 9

Parker

I HAD a reason for looking for him. I wanted to ask about his decision to stop the pancake experiment, but the moment he damn near plows into me, I'm mute.

I'm not prone to not being able to talk. In fact, my ability to think on my feet is one of my strengths.

But standing there, toe to toe with an awkward situation in the flesh, my voice decides to take a vacation to the Bahamas without me.

"Can I help you?"

His voice is deep and rough. He could probably read a cereal box and I'd be content to just stand there and listen to him.

I swallow and try to find my voice. "So I wanted to talk to you about an idea I had."

Yeah, so much for that thinking-on-your-feet thing. Christ, I'm a mess.

He doesn't say anything, which makes things a thousand times more awkward.

"I wrote up a marketing proposal. I zeroed in on key demographics and purchasing behaviors and recommended the best targeting platforms to reach them." I thrust a blue and gold monogrammed folder at him. "It's all here. You should look into it."

It's a long moment before he takes it. "Thanks. I'll look it over later, when I have some time."

I'm not sure what I expected but this wasn't it. It's oddly deflating. "So what am I doing tonight?"

"Talk to Deacon. If Kelsey shows up, follow her lead. They'll get you situated for tonight. I hope you're ready to be busy."

I offer a hesitant smile, unsure how to talk to a man who turned me down for sex. It's so utterly demoralizing. "Okay then."

I turn to go, to escape the narrow hallway with the black and white photos lining the wall, then I stop.

There, right at eye level, is a picture of five men in military uniforms. It's next to the poem of the Fiddler's Green I'd been looking at last night. I'm not sure how I missed this one.

I barely recognize him in the picture. It's his eyes that I notice first, then the shape of his shoulders, the wide frame of his mouth. He looks completely different without his beard. Younger. Maybe a little more hopeful. Less cynical, maybe.

They're standing near a giant cement barrier. There's a drawing of a wolf on it—a grey one—howling at the moon beneath the word "Wolfpack" written in gold block letters.

"This is you?"

There's a darkness in his eyes when I look back over at him. Not shame, though. No, not shame. Something else. A wariness. Even a subtle pride.

"Yeah. Me and the guys I commanded with."

"Where were you?" I'm insanely curious about his life before coming to Durham.

"Iraq. 2009."

He's standing close. Close enough that I can catch a quick scent of him, something spicy and warm and drawing me closer.

But I'm not going to beg.

I'm not playing games with this man. Or any man, for that matter.

"How long were you there?"

"Fifteen months."

I swallow, hoping I'm not about to ask a stupid question. "Why did you enlist?"

"I didn't enlist. I was an officer. I commissioned." His voice rumbles near my ear. I fight to suppress a shiver. I want to lean back, to feel the broad expanse of his chest against me.

"What does that mean?"

"Different legal responsibilities, mostly."

I lift my finger, tracing the edge of the photograph. Like I expect to feel the sand beneath my fingertip. "So why did you sign up?"

"Why do you want to know?"

"I'm curious. About men like you. I had a classmate last semester in my violence class. He argued for things that I can't understand." I lick my bottom lip and try not to look like I want to peel his clothes from his body.

He leans against the wall, his shoulder just beneath the Wolf-pack picture.

"My dad was in. My whole life, I wanted to be like my dad. Be the kind of man I thought he was." His voice is low and smooth. Like honey but with some spice thrown in. "I went to West Point because it was free and I thought it would make me into a man like my dad."

I get the feeling he's humoring me but I'm not about to interrupt. "Did you like it?"

He leans over, straightening one of the pictures. It's of him—I think—in the back of a helicopter. "There was a lot to like. You'd be amazed how hard you can laugh when you're freezing your balls off in a flat-ass downpour after you haven't showered in two weeks."

"I cannot fathom ever not showering for two weeks."

He smiles faintly. "You get used to it. You get used to a lot. The abnormal becomes normal."

"I can't imagine everything was fun."

He swallows and I am enthralled by the movement of his throat. "No. Not all of it."

"Is that why you got out?"

"I left for a lot of reasons." He brushes his finger over my upper arm, near the bruises. "Why don't you?"

"What?"

"Why don't you leave?"

It's my turn to look away, to focus on something else for a moment. I find the only answer that makes sense. "It's complicated."

When he says nothing, I look up at him. He's watching me, not the picture that he's probably seen a thousand times before.

"What?" I can barely push the word out of my throat.

"You surprise me."

"That doesn't happen often? You work in a bar."

His eyes crinkle at the edges and he straightens, the moment that passed between us dissipating like smoke. "Bars are amazingly predictable in their patterns."

"Yeah?"

"You'll see. We're putting you behind the bar tonight. So you can learn a few of the regulars before we set you to the wolves."

I frown at the reference. "Wolves?"

"You've been to frat parties. You know what happens when you mix drinking with underfucked college students."

I lift one eyebrow. "I wouldn't know."

He laughs then and it surprises me. "I'm not entirely sure how to respond to that."

"Well, I know one way you could have," I mumble under my

breath. The disappointment is a tight knot in my chest. What does it say about me that a guy will turn me down?

I turn away and head back up front, away from the unfuckable shame burning over my skin.

"Hey."

He doesn't grab me. Doesn't spin me around and pin me against the wall. Not that I wouldn't mind.

But oh no, not Eli. No, he's a goddamned Boy Scout.

His palm is warm on my back through the t-shirt. I want his hand to slide lower over the small of my back and just stroke my skin.

I want so badly to be touched. Not by anyone. By *him*.

But I don't turn back to face him. I can't.

My life is the perfect lie and I still can't face the reality that maybe, things aren't so perfect and haven't been for a long time.

"I don't know who got into your head and told you that you're unfuckable, but you most assuredly are."

It's a mystery how he read my thoughts so perfectly. "That is the most backhanded compliment I've ever received."

I feel him move behind me. "I've got a million of them."

It's my turn to remain speechless. I don't trust that I won't embarrass myself.

I slip from beneath the warmth of his touch, away from the craving that threatens to consume me.

And step from the light into the darkness.

Eli

I watch her walk away and I'm...intrigued.

But there is something incredibly sad in Parker's words that reveals just how not perfect she really is. And that imperfection is the thing that draws me to her. More than I was before.

Does she really believe that she's…she can't?

She's got to be fucking with me for turning her down last night. Girls like her aren't used to being told no, so she's screwing with me out of revenge.

Has to be.

Because the alternative…it just doesn't line up with the sum of all of my interactions to date with the flora and fauna of this rapidly gentrifying North Carolina town.

I catch Deacon looking at the clock. "No sign of Kels yet?"

Kels is…unpacking a whole lot of stuff from the war. And about the only thing I, or any of us can do is be there when she stumbles and falls and help her back up again.

And hope she's strong enough to get up just once more.

He shakes his head. "Nope. Not seeing that she's read my texts, either."

I glance down at my watch. I've had it since I was a cadet—it was the first thing I bought with my own money at the Cadet Store. It's nothing fancy or super expensive, but I've kept it because I've gotten so used to wearing it, I would feel naked without it.

"Gonna be a busy night then," I mumble. I need to go through the applications and hire new staff. I can afford it. I've been delaying for a couple of reasons, which doesn't make sense now that I've finally brought fresh blood on in the form of Parker.

"You looked like you were having a good chat in the hallway," Deacon says, firing off a text and slipping his phone into his back pocket.

"She was asking about the Army."

He looks at me like I've grown horns. "And you were entertaining those questions?"

"Well, she didn't start talking about how she's a level fifty-two or whatever on *Call of Duty* so she's got that going for her."

He grins. "That's a bonus, all right."

We open the doors in another hour. I'm holding out hope that Kelsey is going to show up as we prep for opening. Parker walks up from where she'd been setting out the small jars with candles in them.

"Deacon is putting me on the floor. Should I be worried?"

When I don't answer and make a show of looking at my phone, she keeps going, not taking the hint that right now, I can't deal with her being in my space, in my head. I need to focus. One problem at a time. I have a really hard time doing that when Parker is around. "Texting Kelsey?"

"She won't answer. She never does." I slide my phone back into my pocket. "If none of us hears from her by midnight, I'll send someone out to her place. Just to be on the safe side."

She frowns. "Why?"

"Why what?"

"Why would you send someone to her place?"

I frown slightly. "To check on her. Why else?"

"But that's not your job. You're her boss, not her father."

I scrub my hand over the back of my neck, unsure how to respond. "I'm just looking out for her. Making sure she's okay. That's what we do."

A strange emotion fills Parker's eyes. Something that reminds me not of loss, but of longing. "Oh."

It takes me a moment to realize that it's not her question that catches me off guard. It's that she can't conceptualize a world where something as basic as checking on a friend is not a unique and foreign concept.

Parker tips her chin and looks up at me, catching me watching her. There is an awareness now, a wariness in her light green eyes.

"What?" I ask quietly.

Whatever passed between us earlier is gone now, leaving simmering sexual tension writhing through the air between us.

Parker presses her lips into a flat line. "Just trying to figure you out, that's all."

"Not a lot of mystery."

"Oh, I beg to differ." There is something sharp and biting in her words. Sharper than I expect from someone as light and fluffy-looking as Parker.

"What, just because I wouldn't fuck on demand the first night we met?" The words are out before I can stop them.

She doesn't flinch away from the harshness of my words. "Maybe you're right about me. Maybe I'm not used to being told no."

Sharp, biting words. I can hear the real pain hiding behind them, cowering in the dark. I take a step closer to her in the dim light. She is pale and soft and prim and proper. She lives in a world that I've run hard and fast from and never looked back.

And yet, like the life I've tried to forget, she's followed me. Into the dark spaces in my head, she's there. Something pure and light amidst the dark, twisted memories I've tried so hard to pretend are anything but.

Unable to stop myself, I reach for her. Her skin is soft beneath my touch. Soft and warm and *real.* It's been so long since I've touched a woman for pure pleasure. But this woman...I keep my touch light, deliberately so.

She doesn't pull away. She leans into my palm, almost nuzzling against it like a kitten waiting to be petted.

Her need to be touched is the single most erotic thing I've ever experienced. It would be so fucking easy to take her back into my office. To lock the door and lower her to my desk and sink inside the welcome I see in her eyes.

But I can't do that. Because it's what she thinks she wants.

It's what she thinks she deserves. And I won't do that to her.

She's worth more than a quick fuck in my office or in the alley behind my bar. "I don't know who made you think you're worth so little," I murmur, "but you're not what they say you are."

I want her to hear me but I don't think she does. She simply turns her lips into my palm and presses them to the rough calluses.

And then there is space between us and my palm is cold and empty without her filling it.

She catches me off guard with her next sentence. "Where does it come from?"

I frown, struggling to find my bearing. "Where does *what* come from?"

"This profound sense of responsibility for the people around you."

"Maybe it's just how I'm wired." I'm uncomfortable with the direction this conversation is heading. I do the looking out and looking in. People don't look into me.

"I've never met anyone wired like you are."

"You don't know me." My throat is tight. I need to get back to my damn end-of-month reports, but instead I'm standing there, worried about one of my employees and under inspection by another.

I feel exposed. Vulnerable. Like she can look at me and see my sins. Some I committed. Others I failed to prevent.

I am hiding in plain sight. Out in the open. Hoping no one ever digs deep into my background, beyond "served in combat". I don't owe the world beyond my commanders *any* explanation for my time in the service, and yet standing there, so close to a woman I refuse to touch, I feel a thousand unwanted emotions.

"You're right. I don't." She takes a step back. "And I think you like it that way. Keep everyone at a distance. Always keep the focus on others, never on yourself." She smiles sadly. "In that, you're just like everyone else in my life."

She slips away, back toward Deacon, where he's waiting to continue briefing her on how to work the floor and place orders with the bartenders.

I'm not exactly sure what just happened here. I feel like I just got my punk card pulled, stamped, and handed back to me.

A shiver of uncertainty slides over my spine as I watch her. I hope Deacon is wrong. That there is nothing more complicated to Parker than a rich girl slumming on Daddy's money.

But I can't shake the feeling that there is more to Parker Hauser than she's let on.

And she might be the biggest mistake I've made since I came here to rebuild my life after leaving the Army and the war behind.

CHAPTER 10

Eli

Kelsey walks in thirty minutes after we open, and for the first time in my life I'm glad the bar is slower than it should be. I'd be pissed but I'm too relieved to see her. She flips her glossy black hair over her shoulder and smiles brightly as she immediately gets to work behind the bar. "Hey. Sorry I scared you. Food poisoning."

I fold my arms over my chest, trying to look like a pissed-off boss. "Yeah? From what? I'd like to avoid praying to the porcelain gods if at all possible."

"Not sure. I ate off one of the new fusion food trucks, and the next thing I know, I'm waking up passed out on the bathroom floor." She looks up at me. "And before you say anything, no I wasn't roofied and yes, I'm sure."

"Well, as long as you're sure." I grin, hiding my worry. "So everything is okay? Did you get that appointment at the VA you were trying to get?"

She slices up an orange with a violence that has me wanting to protect my junk from her rage. "That place is becoming the place that shall not be named. Would it be considered temporary insanity if I just snap one day and burn the entire fucking building to the ground?"

"Since you're discussing it, that qualifies as premeditated, so probably not."

"If I get called 'honey' and asked for my husband's social security number one more time, I'm going to cut a bitch."

Kels would probably do it, too. "I'll start a jail bond fund in your name. Why is it so hard for you to get seen there?"

She cups her breasts and wiggles her hips. "See these? I've got the wrong plumbing for this VA. Turns out, they only know what to do with the boys, and even then, *they* can't get appointments."

"Keep trying. And keep records of all of this. You might need to testify before Congress about this."

She looks at me like I'm fucking cross-eyed. "Sure. And I've got a bridge in Arizona to sell ya. Speaking of which, I might need to adjust my schedule for next semester."

"Sure. Just let me know and we'll make it happen."

She smiles brightly at someone over my shoulder. "Hey! You ready for your first night?"

I follow her gaze to see Parker approaching. She's wearing a plain t-shirt that hugs every curve, and I'm struck by how bright she is in the dim light of the bar. Her hair is tucked behind one ear in a lopsided braid. She must have done that in the bathroom or something because it damn sure wasn't braided an hour ago.

There are a million filthy things I could do with that braid. I have the sudden urge to lift that braid off her neck and press my lips to her skin. To feel her tip her chin to one side and trace my tongue over her pulse and capture her sigh.

I want this woman. I want the promise I see in her eyes. I want to feel her need...me. Just me.

Not the owner of The Pint. Not the former soldier. Not the tatted-out bartender.

Just me.

But I won't do that to her. Because she wanted to fuck for the wrong reasons. And until I'm sure she's looking at me, really *me*, I can't...I *won't* cross that line, no matter how badly my dick might resent my principled stance.

"I'm ready. I hope," Parker says brightly. She's not even dealing with customers yet.

"You'll be fine. Just remember no one has the right to put their hands on you. Standing order in this place." She points to a sign behind the bar and Parker's eyes widen as she just notices it.

"How about that? That's pretty cool."

"There're a lot of cool things about this place," Kelsey says. "I'll be right back. We need more Jack Daniels."

Kelsey disappears into the basement leaving me alone with Parker. Her smile fades just a little, and just like that, I see the girl in the alley once more, asking for things that she doesn't really want because she thinks it will fix what ails her.

I hate that I can't fix it. That I can't lift her chin and kiss the sadness from her eyes. And I don't want her to see this side of me. The helplessness that twists inside me when I can't fix what's wrong with the people in my life.

"Are you okay?" It's almost a statement rather than a question. Almost.

She looks away. "Just things I'd rather avoid not letting me avoid them."

"Things like the cause of this?" I reach across the bar and brush my thumb gently, so gently beneath the bruise that she's done a better job of concealing today.

Her lips twist into a humorless smile. "You're a pretty good guesser."

"I'm good with people. It's part of the job description."

"Is that bartender or soldier?" she asks softly.

"Both. The Army is a people business."

"So's running a bar."

"Pretty much." She brushes her braid off her shoulder, exposing the shimmering skin of her throat. I am drawn to it, to her. To the vulnerability in her. The strength.

"You're glad she's here," Parker says quietly.

"Obviously. Otherwise, tonight was going to be really hectic."

"Nice try." She slips her hands into the front pocket of her jeans, angling her body slightly toward me. "You're glad she's safe. You're genuinely glad."

"Why wouldn't I be? She works for me."

"That's not it. There's something more. You love her. But not sexually. Like she's one of your soldiers."

I open my mouth, then close it again. I'm not used to having someone poking around inside my head. "So?"

Her smile is shielded. "It's nice. Seeing that you care about your people."

I clear my throat. "Comments like that make me want to get you drunk and hear your life's story."

"Well, I was thinking about getting drunk before my shift really got going."

I can't help but grin. "Nervous?"

"A little bit. I'm not nearly as good with people as you are."

"I find that hard to believe."

She toys with the edge of her braid. "A little alcohol goes a long way to loosen a girl up." Her eyes widen and her mouth forms a surprised "O". "That came out wrong. What I meant was..."

"I know." I don't want to think about her that first night. About how soft she was against the hard, wet brick. About the want I felt in her body.

Or the revulsion I felt when I realized she was trying to hurt herself to hurt someone else.

"You never asked me for any references," she's saying when I can focus on her words. "How do you know I'm not some klepto-arsonist-in-training?"

"You don't look like a klepto-arsonist."

"And you know what one looks like?"

"Funny you should mention it, but yes, actually I do." She's smiling now, and the sadness I saw in her eyes earlier is fading beneath her rampant curiosity.

She leans forward on the bar, braced on her elbows. "Oh, do tell."

"This kid, Meyers, was in my platoon. Things started turning up missing out of the barracks a few weeks after we deployed. He was a skinny little fuck. Got hooked on meth, started stealing and eventually caught his entire block of the LSA on fire."

"I'm sorry, you lost me at 'LSA'."

"Life Support Area. Sorry. Where everyone lived on the big bases overseas."

She makes a noise. "And what happened to young Meyers?"

"He ran away. Went home on midtour leave and never came back. We ended up dropping him from the rolls."

She flinches, then frowns. I tuck that little piece of information away for later. "You just let him go?"

I shrug. "Sometimes it's easier to let people go than to fight to make them do something they don't want to. Or, something you don't want to do. I would have had to court-martial him if he hadn't gone AWOL. Him leaving saved us both from doing something we didn't want to do."

She runs her index finger over the edge of her thumbnail thoughtfully, as if she's contemplating whether I'm telling her the truth or not. It's amazing how much energy and motion is contained in such a small package.

She finally looks back up at me. "What a fascinating life you must have led in the Army," she whispers.

"You can't make up the stories we tell." The funny stories, the shit people won't believe, those I don't mind talking about. The rest?

The rest I want to leave buried in the moon dust of the desert sand.

CHAPTER 11

Parker

"I'm sorry, you need a what?"

"A blowjob."

"I'm pretty sure I'd need to know your name before we get that intimate." Half of me can't believe I just said that. The other half can't figure out why on earth I'm still standing here.

Oh yeah, because I'm a waitress. Which apparently means pretending I'm fuckable to half the clientele in The Pint tonight. I thought I wanted to get tips as a point of pride. Now they just feel like dirty money.

Now if he'd asked for a hundred-dollar bottle of whiskey, I could have at least had a point of reference for what he was asking for. But right now, I'm pretty far out of my league, and I'm not entirely sure the guy isn't screwing with me.

He's like a real-life dick pic standing in front of me, offering himself up like some kind of prize at the carnival freak show.

I'm really wishing that the missing waitress had shown up and that I wasn't running the entire floor my first night on the job.

Mr. Blowjob grins up at me and it's half a leer. "It's a drink, Tits."

I roll my eyes. "Last time I checked, my name wasn't Tits McGee."

Mr. Blowjob rocks back on two legs of his chair and grins. "I'm impressed you got the reference. Most girls around here wouldn't lower themselves to watching *Anchorman.*"

"Yeah, well, that just goes to show you what you know about the girls around here." I sniff and resist the urge to tell him to go fuck himself. I don't need the tip but I do need my self-respect. "About that drink?"

He chuckles. "I'll pass on the blowjob. Glenfiddich 14 Year Reserve if you have it." I lift both eyebrows and say nothing as I scratch the word "blowjob" from my notepad. My life has gotten so strange.

"I'll be right back with that," I say. "Anything else?"

"A menu? I think I want something to eat."

Since he didn't say he wanted me for dinner, I won't throw a salt shaker at his head. I can't quite get beyond the whole rapid transition between the blowjob comment and his normal ordering of high-end Scotch and food.

Maybe I'm just new and I'll get used to the ADHD customers. Or something.

I walk up to the bar in time to see Kelsey stalking off. Deacon looks like he wants to hit something. Or someone.

I'm almost hesitant to ask him if he's got the whiskey, but I figure I need to do this. Maybe his attitude is some kind of new employee test or something.

"It's in the vault." And he tosses me keys. Like I'm supposed to just find my way into the basement. Pretty sure that's how horror movies start.

"Y'all are seriously trusting around here."

Deacon grins. "Looks like you figured us out. We murder all the new help and hide the bodies in the cellar."

"Not funny." I'm not a coward, not by a long shot. But the look in Deacon's eyes pushes me back like a physical force. He's joking and yet, it doesn't feel like he's joking.

I lift my chin against his stare. "You look at customers like that and no one will buy anything from you."

His eyes are brittle and cold. "You clearly haven't been paying attention. Girls like you love being treated like shit by guys like me. You think you're better than us but you just bend over and take whatever we dish out."

"And aren't you just a little ray of sunshine?" I manage to keep the words light but his words sting. Because that's exactly how I've ended up in this bar to begin with.

I wanted to be used and discarded.

Just not by Deacon.

He doesn't move for a long moment, and I rapidly contemplate my own mortality. Then he grunts and turns away, leaving me to wonder if I've made a new enemy.

I head to the narrow stairway that leads to the basement.

I hate cellars. I hate the rough, cold brick beneath my hands. I hate the shadows licking the walls and crawling up my spine.

"This is a freaking hazing event," I mumble as I walk down into the darkness. I need the sound of my voice to drown out the creeping silence. "So this is quite possibly the dumbest thing I've ever done. I can't believe that I'm walking down into a strange basement, looking for some stupid whiskey. Amazing how my life fortunes have changed, all because someone decided his penis was something I *needed* to see."

I run my fingers along the shelves, looking for the whiskey. "Jesus, he has Glenfiddich Snow Phoenix." Not only does Eli know enough about whiskey to have it on hand, he must also have the resources to get it. Snow Phoenix can run into the thousands of dollars a bottle; it's not for the hobbyist. "I'm officially impressed,"

I murmur. The shelves are lined with some seriously high-end whiskey.

"Glad to hear it."

There is no way to mute the unladylike scream that tears out of my throat. My heart staggers and my eyes instantly tear up.

It takes me a full thirty seconds to inhale and realize that it's Eli standing in front of me. Big, beautiful Eli, who knows instantly what he's done. Whose hands are on my shoulders, cradling my neck. Who is whispering nonsense in my ear that I can't really hear over the pounding of my blood in my head.

I don't move away. I probably should. But I haven't been scared like this in...I can't even remember how long. I lean my head against his chest and will my heart to slow down.

I want to stay here. Right here in the moment with the black-inked arms wrapped around me, breathing him in.

I *want* in ways that ache deep inside me.

Correction. I *wanted*. But he said no, and I'll be damned if I'm going to beg.

Because there is a life waiting for me on the other side of my so-called internship here at The Pint.

I lean away, putting at least a nominal amount of space between us.

"I didn't mean to scare you." His words are rough, his words laced with dark concern.

"Sneaking up on someone in a cellar says otherwise. It isn't generally a good way to go about *not* scaring them."

He grins and it does something to his features. He's no longer all hard edges and black lines. I can see a hint of the young officer in the picture on his wall. It dawns on me then that there is more than class separating us. He's got a lifetime of experience I will never have.

"You okay now?" He takes a step back, releasing me from the compulsion that draws me closer to him.

He's drawn me since that first night, when I decided I wanted to try to let go, to really let go. I want to know what it feels like to fly. To let go of the constraints that my world has on me.

"Sure." I look back over my shoulder at the whiskey and bourbon lining the shelves behind me. "That's some really expensive whiskey you have down here," I say when I can sound even remotely like myself. "Do you have any 14 Year Glenfiddich? Mr. Blowjob upstairs might have a heart attack if I bring him a glass of Snow Phoenix."

He leans across me then. I am fascinated by the movement of sinew beneath the tight lines of his skin. It takes every ounce of control I have not to trace my fingers over the black lines that follow the veins beneath skin that's stretched tightly over his muscle and bone.

I want his hands on me. I want to feel his mouth, his beard against my skin.

But I'm not going to beg. I have some pride.

"Did he really ask you for a blowjob?"

"If I say yes, are you going to rip out his spine? Because you know that wouldn't be good for business."

He smiles again. It's like he's constantly surprised by the things that come out of my mouth. In a good way. Which is rare.

"Only if you can't handle it."

"Nothing surprises me anymore."

I tip my head and look up at him. He hasn't dropped his arm. I'm effectively boxed in. Where, had he willingly lent me the use of his penis the other night, I would be perfectly happy to remain.

But he didn't. And I'm trying really hard not to take it personally.

I might be a little bitter. Just a teeny bit.

"Can I ask you a question?" My mouth is dry. He makes a noise that I will take as a yes before I lose my nerve. "Why did you really say no?"

Eli

THE MINUTE the words are out of her mouth, heat flashes over my skin.

Why did I say no? She's been practically begging for me to fuck her since I met her. But my goddamned moral code won't let me. I can't.

She's worth more than that.

I can't say those words to her. Not without sounding like a sexist asshole. "I already told you."

"That's not a good enough answer." She's not going to let me off the hook this time. This whole scenario just got awkward as hell.

I retreat to the safety of sarcasm. "Never really had that problem before?"

She licks her bottom lip and I suddenly want to do nothing else for the rest of the night but nibble on her. She doesn't answer. I fill the silence because there is so much more I want to do with her. "No, you probably have a different problem altogether." My voice is tight. I want to slip her out of her clothes. To press my body against hers. To feel her warmth penetrate the cold, dead space inside me.

"What problem do you think I have?" Her voice is hushed and strained.

Everything about her is just there, within my reach. It would be so easy to lift my finger and trace the scattered beat of her pulse. I could place my lips over it again and feel her shiver.

In truth, there's no good reason for me to hold back.

I take a step closer, moving into her space, close enough that I can feel the heat from her body.

"Do you always get what you want?" I whisper, lowering my head until my mouth is a breath from hers. Right there.

She's sober tonight. Unlike the other night.

So am I.

"No." Her answer comes out as a breathy huff against my mouth.

"Don't lie." *An officer will not lie, steal, nor cheat.* But she's not an officer.

And neither am I. Not anymore.

"I don't lie." There's a fierce insistence in those three whispered words.

My lips curl at the edges. "What haven't you gotten that you wanted?"

Hope is a fragile thing in my chest. If she says the words, if she so much as breathes the single word I want to hear, I will drop to my knees in gratitude and thank a God I don't believe in.

"Your penis, for starters."

The laugh rips free, surprising me. I lower my head to her forehead, slipping my hand over her hip to the small of her back. I give in to the urge to press her body to mine, savoring the brief human contact.

"Do you always say things before you think them?"

A moment ago, all I'd wanted in the whole world was for her to whisper my name so I could lay her across my bar and do filthy things to her and now I can't stop laughing.

"It wasn't that funny," she mutters. She's hurt. Or maybe a little embarrassed. Either way, she's not enjoying the moment any longer.

I cup her cheek to stop her from leaving. "Don't go."

She hesitates and looks away, her cheeks flushed.

"Why not?"

I have a ridiculous urge to keep her there. To hold on to this fleeting moment.

"The truth," I whisper. Why, of all the bars she could have gone into, and all the bartenders who would have been happy to fuck her six ways from Sunday, she came into my bar. Why she picked me. "I need to know. I need to know why you picked me that night."

It's a stupid insecurity. A holdover from my days on the football team at West Point, when girls would drop their panties because of what I was, not who I was. I need to know. Know that she picked me. Not who she thinks I am. Not out of some twisted desire to screw the brains out of the fucked-up vet.

"I wanted to let go," she whispers.

"Of what?"

She won't look at me now. I can feel the change in her, the shame creeping up her skin like a flush.

"Everything. I wanted to just close my eyes and feel and forget."

"Forget what?"

"Everything." She closes her eyes, her word tight and tense. "And I thought you might be perfect to help me do that."

I want to erase it all. The shame I see on her face, the pain I hear in that single word. I want to know what caused her to need...this.

I kiss her then because it's the only thing I can think to do. Providing a balm against the hurt, if not erasing it.

She is softer than I imagined and more hesitant. Her breath catches the moment my lips brush hers.

I am deliberately slow. My tongue slides, flicking, then nipping, then finally tugging at her full bottom lip. Any surprise I feel is buried beneath a sharp pang of desire that burns a path straight to my cock. This is lazy and languid, like a summer afternoon on a porch swing.

I want this to go on forever. I want to lean her back against the two-thousand-dollar whiskey and lift her legs around my hips. I want to stroke her and watch her let go beneath my touch. I lean back a little, sucking on her bottom lip a moment longer before I release her.

"Guess I was right," she whispers.

I smile against her mouth. She's good on the ego, that's for damn sure.

"I should go. Mr. Blowjob is waiting for his whiskey."

I stroke my thumb across her cheek gently, not quite ready to let her go. Because I have questions, questions about her words that drew me to her from the dark, where I was checking the inventory.

"Whatever you're hiding from, you can hide here."

Of the thousand reactions I expected, resignation bordering on defeat was not one of them. "Thank you. But I can't hide forever."

"Why not?"

She shakes her head and looks away. "Ask me again sometime?"

I let her go, watching her climb the stairs carrying a bottle of Glenfiddich 14 Year Bourbon Barrel Reserve.

Whoever Mr. Blowjob is, he has expensive taste.

Of course, he's going to have to take blowjobs off the menu.

Because despite all of my good intentions, Parker is drawing me out of the dark, where I've been doing my own hiding. I've hidden in plain sight for six years, drawing me into the light, where I risk everything I've built here.

All for a fleeting taste of belonging...in a way I haven't allowed myself to belong since everything went to hell downrange.

CHAPTER 12

Parker

IT IS NEARLY two a.m. and I am dead on my feet. The bar is finally slowing down, thank God.

"You look ready to collapse."

If I close my eyes, I can still feel Eli's mouth on mine, the soft scrape of his beard against my skin as his lips moved against me. I can think of nothing better than curling up in bed right now and letting my brain take that thought to some very interesting places. Well, maybe I can think of something better. But that's assuming I'd make it home to my own bed. I'm so tired, I'm seriously considering sleeping in the car.

I haven't been this tired in…I can't remember the last time. Maybe not ever.

Eli motions toward Mr. Glenfiddich with his chin. "You're being paged. Has he behaved?"

I press my lips into a flat line. "Well, he hasn't grabbed my ass or called me Tits McGee again, so does that count?"

"Well, it's Saturday, so yes, I guess that counts."

"What does Saturday have to do with anything?"

He shrugs. "Nothing, really." He shifts then, and stuffs his hands in his back pockets. "You don't have to go over there. Your shift is up."

There's a strange silence surrounding us. It's like the world is passing us by, leaving us alone in this quiet, not quite bubble. "Do you ever sleep?"

"Sure."

"That's a non-answer," I mumble, half to myself.

He looks at me funny then, an odd expression in his dark grey eyes. "Yes, Parker, I sleep."

I'm too tired to be able to read between the lines. I'm not sure if he's flirting with me or not. I might just be sleep-deprived enough to claim impairment and throw myself at him again. Just to see if he would still say no the second time around. "I'm going to go finish up with Mr. Glenfiddich, then I'll head out."

"Have fun."

Oh, I'm sure it will be a blast handing Mr. Expensive Tastes in Whiskey his tab for just shy of five hundred dollars. And I bet he's not even got a light buzz. Awful expensive way to spend an evening.

"Ready to call it a night?" I ask, handing him the small slip of paper inside a real leather bill envelope.

Eli has some strange propensities. Real leather doesn't make sense for a run-of-the-mill bar—it's too expensive but in that subtlety, he's signaling class to the people who notice details like that. People who drink five hundred dollar a glass whiskey. And even if it is more durable, it's a subtle touch that most of the crowd in here wouldn't notice.

"Sure." He slips what I assume is his credit card into the envelope but when I open it, I see a business card. Cream, with canted edges. And dear lord do I sound like a weirdo obsessed with *American Psycho*.

I hand the card back to him. "Sorry. Not interested." I stop myself. I'm not going to say thank you for attention I didn't ask for and had actually already said no to.

"I'm a journalist. I'm writing a piece about veterans returning to civilian life."

I set the card on the table when he refuses to take it. "I'm not a veteran."

"No, but you're working at a bar filled with them."

"So?" There's something nagging at the base of my spine. A cold warning, slithering over my skin.

"So, I wanted to interview you as a baseline—see what civilians think about working here. Drinking here. Playing here." He reaches back into his wallet and hands over his credit card while he talks.

"I'll have to talk to the owner. I'm sure he'd like to be aware of any media presence."

"That's Eli Winter, right?"

I know better than to say anything that can be misconstrued or quoted out of context. Life is funny that way. While other kids were learning how to ride a bike, I was being coached on how to act in front of the media. I suppose that's the very definition of First World problems, isn't it? "Sure. I'll be right back with your final bill."

Despite my misgivings, I take the card and slip away, into the empty shadows toward the bar. Deacon swipes the credit card through the card reader.

"What's that about?"

"Reporter. Wants to do a story on the bar."

Deacon looks up at me sharply. He says nothing for a long moment, letting the uncomfortable silence drag on. It feels like forever before he swipes the card again and hands it back to me.

It's only when he hands it back to me that I bother to look down and read Mr. Glenfiddich's name. Ryan Pool. Mr. Pool has an exceptionally large bill. I wonder if he's expensing the alcohol tonight as research for his story. And what accountant is going to be stupid enough to fall for that.

"Eli is pretty careful who he talks to." I'm not so new that I can't read between the lines of Deacon's quiet statement.

It makes sense that Eli would be a private person. Everything about him is reserved, despite the public-facing persona I've read about in the local paper. The details are generic. No sense of the man behind the bar. Just enough detail to fit into the comfortable professional veteran stereotype the American public thanks for their service.

I can imagine the reporter is curious. That makes two of us. But I'm not looking for a scoop or a story.

I never was.

I look across the bar. Eli is talking to a couple of guys. I recognize one of them as Josh from class last semester. He was fun to argue with.

There are worry lines around Eli's eyes now, a strain around his mouth. But there is something else in his eyes.

Something I would give anything to see looking back at me.

Eli

NOAH LOOKS LIKE SHIT. But I can't tell if it's because he's using or because he's not. Pain pills are funny like that. And I'm not his fucking commander. "When's the last time you slept?"

"I'm good, man. I started doing this meditation shit before Beth left on her trip."

"Is it helping?"

He shrugs and offers a lopsided half-grin that's mostly forced. "Well, I'm getting some sleep as opposed to none."

"When's Beth coming back?" I need to know how long to keep

Josh checking on him. How long I need to be on edge for another one of my adopted band of merry miscreants.

Josh and Noah are two of the guys I met through The Pint. They haven't been coming in as regularly anymore, but they will always be mine to watch over. The shit we carry doesn't magically disappear when you get a girlfriend. But they're both trending positive these days, unlike Caleb, who hasn't really learned anything from his latest brush with alcohol poisoning.

"Pick her up tomorrow." He rubs the back of his neck. "I still can't believe she landed this consulting gig."

Parker catches my eye, and I watch her hand Mr. Blowjob his receipt. I don't miss the way she's careful not to touch him. She's exhausted, but she's too stubborn to quit.

And I really need her to clock out for the night. To give me space from the need that seems to be overwhelming my rational thought process capabilities.

"You hired Parker Hauser?"

"You know her?" I don't like the tone in Noah's voice.

"Yeah, she's been in a bunch of my classes."

It's amazing how defensive his comment made me, almost instantly. "She needed a summer internship. She's doing fine, too. She made it through the first night."

He grins and it's the first genuine smile I've seen on his face since he got sober. "Okay, I'll admit I'm a little impressed. She didn't strike me as the hard-working waitress type."

I say nothing, watching her work.

Deacon rings the bell for last call and Noah heads out. Mr. Blowjob hands Parker something. I hope it's a tip and not his phone number.

She turns away and starts picking up glasses on a nearby table. She looks dead on her feet.

"You don't make it a habit of staying up this late?"

She offers me a tired grin. "There's a world of difference

between staying up partying and staying up working. I have newfound respect for you people."

I don't flinch at her use of *you people*. I might have, that first night I met her. When I was convinced she was royalty out to play with the commoners. Now? The more time I spend around her, the more I feel like she's...like me.

Just looking for a place to belong.

"You get used to it."

She tips her chin and looks up at me. "How?"

I shrug. "Got used to not sleeping well on deployment. Never really readjusted."

A shadow flitters across her eyes. Lightning fast and then it's gone, leaving only the shadow of fatigue. "I'm not sure what to say to that."

"Just don't say 'thank you for your service'."

"I've heard that some vets don't like that." She finishes stacking glasses on her tray and straightens. "Why don't you?"

"You and all your questions." I brush the tip of her nose with my index finger. "It's a long story, best shared over copious amounts of alcohol."

"I'll take a rain check." She frowns then, and pauses. "Oh, so Mr. Blowjob? He's a reporter. Wants to do a story on this place."

I am instantly still. The ice that shelters my heart from the world spreads through my guts. "What did you tell him?" My words are thick. Lodged somewhere in the vicinity of my heart.

Hoping her next words don't carry betrayal.

She hands me his business card. "I told him that was up to you."

Relief is hot and cold all at once, flashing across my skin. "Thank you. For checking with me first." I drop the card into a small box near the register where I put the rest of the cards people leave.

She shrugs. "It's no biggie. I learned a long time ago that the media aren't your friends."

There's more there in those quiet, tired words. But tonight isn't the time. And the bar isn't the place. "Are you going to be all right to get home?"

"I'm tired, not drunk."

"You didn't answer the question."

She lifts her chin and studies me quietly for a moment. All I can think about is how she tasted earlier. How she felt beneath my fingertips.

How much I want to touch her again.

"I'll be okay. I don't live that far from here."

It would be so easy to ask her to come upstairs with me after the bar closes. To draw her close to me and just feel her body against mine.

It's such a basic fantasy. Nothing sexual. Nothing twisted. Just the feeling of two bodies, skin to skin, breathing together in the darkness.

And sweet baby Jesus, when did I turn into a fucking warrior poet who wants to snuggle? Keeping track of everyone has turned me into an old man.

"Where'd you go just then?" she asks.

"Sorry. Thinking about the close-out report I have to do before I can crash."

"You don't have someone that does that for you?"

I shake my head. "Nah. It's easier this way."

"Except when you want to sleep or do other things after the bar closes."

I don't resist the easy smile that slides across my mouth. "I don't really have a good response for that."

She sets the final empty glass on her tray and straightens. "That actually raises an interesting point. Can I swing in after the bar closes and ask you some questions about who you hire and why?"

"Tonight probably isn't good. Five minutes ago, you were dead on your feet." The reporter's card is a lead weight in my hand. I hate that the suspicions are there, dancing at the edge of my thoughts. Taunting me with what-ifs that are anything but good.

She makes a warm sound in the back of her throat. I am almost lost in what that sound does to me.

"Good point. I'll write some things up so they're more coherent."

She turns back to the bar, bringing Deacon the rest of the glasses.

It's a good thing it's closing time. I need some goddamned distance from this woman in tight jeans who is playing hell on my imagination.

I let my thoughts wander, thinking about the feel of her skin. The taste of her lips and the warm slide of her breath across my tongue.

Because if I don't, the insidious fear that the reporter's card has raised in the back of my mind will consume me. And I know what that feels like already.

I left the war and its demons behind in Iraq.

There's no reason to resurrect them now that I'm home.

CHAPTER 13

Parker

MY PHONE DRAGS me out of what is quite possibly the best sleep I've ever had. I've been completely dead to the world, judging by my alarm clock, for six hours.

Which means the sun is up and I'm late for...oh wait, the semester is over.

No class. No appointments.

I stretch until my spine pops.

Then my phone angrily reminds me that whoever is calling needs my attention.

Is it too much to hope that it's Eli? That maybe he needs some early morning help at the bar that could get me out of my apartment and alone with him?

Being alone with Eli is pretty high up on my priorities list. Right up there with avoiding Davis for a little longer. I should ask Kelsey for advice. She'd probably just tell me how to stab him, though. I'm mostly convinced she's joking.

94

The possibility of being alone with Eli today…

Dear lord the man can kiss.

I roll toward the phone and drop my head to the mattress. It's my father.

And he's already called three times this morning. He's often disappointed in me but rarely does he blow my phone up like this. Which means I'm standing on ice that has already spider-webbed beneath my feet.

And damn it, I had been in the middle of a really, really great dream.

"Hi, Dad."

"Do you have a drug problem that I should know about?"

I roll onto my back and stare at the ceiling. "Yes, Daddy. I was passed out in an alley getting fucked by a homeless person when you called."

I slap my hand over my mouth. The silence on the other end lets me know that those words actually slipped free instead of me just thinking them.

I brace for the storm of his disappointment. I've heard everything before. All spoken quietly. How my mother would be ashamed of me. How Davis isn't going to want me if I'm a liability with the press. I have to learn to keep my mouth shut or I'll hurt his reelection chances.

The way he talks about Mom isn't the way I remember her. He paints her to be so stoic and calm. I remember us sneaking ice cream at midnight when I couldn't sleep and telling jokes only we got.

Losing my mom changed him. I don't even lie to myself that he loves me anymore. He loves the idea of me. And I think he hates that I remind him of my mom.

I've become a trophy for him. And marrying Davis is a huge cache for him to add to his prestige among his peers.

The silence continues. He must really be pissed if he's not yelling.

"I'm not amused," he says quietly. "Davis needs you at the fundraiser this afternoon and since you won't answer his calls..."

He doesn't have to threaten me. His request is enough that I'll comply. I have to. Because he's asked me to.

"Is there any chance he could do this without me? I really don't feel well."

"No. This is a very big deal with a wealthy campaign contributor. She wants the family values front and center. Any hint of issues between you and Davis puts things at risk."

I press my lips together to bite back the hurt that returns with all the force of a category five storm. God, how I want to break free of all of the pressure of being the future wife to the heir to a political dynasty on par with the Bushes and the Clintons and the Kennedys.

Poor little rich girl, right?

"Did you hear me?" His voice is jarring, grating against my ear.

"Yes, sir."

"I'll see you this afternoon." Just like that, his tone changes. Softens. I remember he used to talk to me like that before my mom died.

I hang up as soon as I can without saying anything else. I miss her terribly. I roll into one of my pillows, wondering if everything would be different if she hadn't died and left me completely alone.

My phone vibrates. I dread looking at it.

I flip it over.

Despite the weight from my father's order, my heart skips a little bit in my chest when I see Eli's text.

I'm at the office doing reports if you want to come in.

For research, of course.

I have a reason to get up. To get dressed. And to step out into the light.

I text him back. *I have to shower first.*

I see the little bubbles indicating he's responding. *Want me to wash your back?*

My throat is instantly dry. I press my thighs together. Tightly. *I wouldn't say no to that.*

I see the little bubbles again. Then they disappear. Then they're back.

Then gone again.

Come to the office. We'll be more productive there.

Coward. Followed by a smiley face emoji. Because I can't help myself, and teasing him feels so much better than wallowing in my own self-pity.

I'll see you when you get here.

I can't figure out why he's backing down but I suddenly very much want to be in the office. With him.

And please dear lord let him be alone. I close my eyes for a moment, remembering his mouth on mine last night. His gentleness surprised me. So had the heat that had spiked through my body the moment his lips touched mine.

My hand resting on my belly drifts lower, pressing between my legs, hoping to ease the ache that thinking about him brings to a fierce intensity. I want his hand between my thighs. His fingers spreading the moisture over my slick flesh. His mouth sucking on me as his fingers slip inside me, stroking me. Petting me. Oh god I want this. I want him.

I don't want to move. I don't want to face the reality of my life.

I want the fantasy.

I'd give it all up to stay in the fantasy. Everything. My car. My father's name. My life.

But that's not how life works for girls like me. My father would never let me go. And Davis? His pride would never survive the tabloid scandals of his being jilted.

It's better to just enjoy my temporary escape.

I finally crawl out of bed. An evil thought races through my brain as I reach for my phone.

I send Eli a final text.

Heading to the gym for yoga. Be at the office in two hours or so.

I shower quickly and head out, smiling to myself. Wondering if the seed I've planted is taking root.

God, I hope so.

Eli

PARKER'S TEXT has left me annoyed and aroused. Which is an unusual combination for me.

And thanks to Parker's yoga pants visual, my brain is no longer focused on anything even remotely professional. Thank god the office door is already closed because my cock is pushing against my jeans in a painfully erect way.

There's something illicit about slipping my cock out of my pants beneath my desk, squeezing it, pretending that it's Parker touching me, Parker stroking me.

Fuck, I need this. I close my eyes, pulling gently on my cock, imagining Parker's warm, sweet mouth sucking gently on the tip. My balls tighten as I stroke myself harder, tighter, needing it to be Parker that's riding me to release.

My release is violent and sudden. My stomach clenches and I double over, the cotton of my t-shirt capturing everything.

Talk about a good time to live upstairs. And an even better time for keeping a clean change of clothes in your office.

I clean everything up and run my laundry upstairs, still utterly distracted by Parker's text.

Back in my office I stare at my computer screen a long time, not really noticing anything but the blinking cursor on my financial reports.

I spot the folder Parker handed me in my inbox. Curious, I open it, wondering just what she recommends for brand awareness and expansion.

I'm impressed inside of the first page. She's got detailed analytics of whiskey drinkers *broken down by brand*, mind you, in the Triangle and surrounding area. She ran an analysis of everyone connected to our social media page. Even more, she's highlighted ways to convert online interactions into real-world sales.

She highlights how to use event targeting—like the private event I'm serving at tonight—to generate an audience in the local area. I'm amazed she did all this and this was without even knowing that I'm scheduled at three local events. When the hell did she have time to do this?

I'm beyond impressed by the detailed plan. And it's a nice distraction from my cock's growing obsession with her.

Who the hell am I kidding? It's not the baser part of my anatomy that's interested in her.

I try to focus on the drink list for the private party over in Chapel Hill that I need to be set up at in six hours. One of the presidents of the university is having some fundraiser or something or other. He wants to highlight local businesses and I managed to secure the opportunity.

Except that I keep circling back to Parker. And not just to the idea of her naked and slippery and wet. I want to know what she's running from. Who's hurt her.

I want her to trust me with that information. Trust me enough to let me walk with her in the darkness of whatever she's running from.

"Now that doesn't look like it's a very good time."

I must have fallen into a time warp for the time to have flown by that quickly, but Parker's voice is a welcome distraction. The sight of her is even more welcome. She's standing in the doorway, her body wrapped in a pair of yoga tights and a plum wrap over a thin tank.

I want to thank whatever powers there might be for those tight little yoga pants. I think I might have to pick up the activity if it involves getting to see Parker in those pants more often. I'd love nothing more than to draw my hands over her smooth, rounded hips and feel her soften beneath my touch.

I'd definitely downward dog for a chance at that. Jesus, how does any man go to yoga classes and not walk out with a raging hard-on after every session?

"I was reading over your analytics," I say, needing the distraction away from my business, which might not exist in another six months if I can't turn this shit around.

"And?"

"You did an amazing job with this. How did you do all this without having access to my social media accounts?" I try to play it cool, but I'm off-kilter right now.

I'm blaming her yoga pants because it's easier to fall into the distraction of her luscious little body.

"I created a similar business page and used its insights to develop potential markets for you." She sits. "It wasn't very hard. Anyone with a basic understanding of Google analytics can figure this stuff out."

"And you did it for free? Do you know how much you could charge people for this information?"

She nods. "I wanted to get better at analytics so I've got a better chance at being accepted into an executive management program."

My dick is all too happy to have me stare, even though I'm genuinely trying to be a responsible adult in this interaction.

I'm failing. But at least I'm trying, right? "You mean there are more of you who know how to do this stuff?"

She surprises me by leaning against my desk. Close enough that if I don't move my arm, I'll be brushing up against her ass.

Which I really, really want to do.

She's looking down at me, and all I can think about is dragging her into my lap. I can't decide if she's being deliberately provocative or is honestly that clueless about what she's doing.

If I go for provocative, does that mean I can touch her? Give in to her demands?

I'm ready to fucking beg. Goddamn it, why didn't I take what she offered that first night?

Parker is a lot of things but clueless isn't one of them. What would she do if I slide my hand over her hip and tug her, just a little, to see if she'd crawl into my lap?

Instead, I clear my throat. Adulting, right? "So what else do you recommend?"

That's an adult-type question to ask, isn't it? I'm honestly not sure at this point because all of my blood has focused on one area of my anatomy that's begging her with every beat of my heart to touch me.

She takes out a notebook and an expensive-looking pen. "I think you need to do social media better but you also need to capitalize on your traffic here. You can fill out this form with Google and have your business listed. Then you can re-target special events at people who come here regularly and people *who are like* people who come here regularly. It could increase your foot traffic by fifteen percent a week, depending on your marketing budget."

She looks up when I haven't spoken. I realize I'm staring.

"What?" she asks.

"Why hasn't this executive program accepted you already? You're too damn smart for them not to grab you up."

Her lips form a small bow. I've discovered this is her thinking expression. It's fucking adorable. "Maybe I'm trying to see if they're smart enough to want me."

"Touché." I suck in a hard breath at the erotic innuendo in those simple words. "Why not just ask your father to help you out? Isn't he well-connected?"

She flushes then and looks down at her hands. A little too quickly. "I don't want to talk about it, if it's all the same to you."

I reach for her then, unable to resist what is right in front of me.

I'm not exactly certain of my plan until I've tugged her into my lap and am looking up into her eyes. "No," I whisper, dragging my thumb across her bottom lip. "It's not all the same to me. Not this time."

Because I can do nothing less, I draw her closer, lifting her knees until they slide around my hips in the narrow office chair. Her skin is soft and warm beneath my fingertips. Her throat barely contains her racing pulse. My thumb slides over the edge of her jaw near her ear, then down her arm. The bruises are fading. "You can't keep hiding from whatever you're running from."

"Telling you about it doesn't help."

"You'd be surprised." I slide my thumb over her skin again. A gentle caress.

"Why do you need to know so much about me?" There is fear in that simple question.

I tug her mouth down to mine then, brushing my lips over hers. "Because I don't sleep with people I can't trust."

CHAPTER 14

Parker

I CLOSE my eyes the moment his lips slip over mine. I can't get used to the softness of his beard against my skin, no matter how often it brushes gently against my cheek. I love the taste of this man. The feel of being surrounded, consumed. He nudges me, urging me to open.

It's a simple request. One I'm all too happy to grant.

It was a gamble, moving so close to him. Daring him to deny what has been burning between us since that first night.

Daring him to turn me away, and hoping, praying that he wouldn't do it again.

I need him in this moment. I need to forget about my father and the rest of this afternoon and the rest of my life.

I need to lose myself in this kiss. This touch. This breathless moment that sweeps me up and tears me apart.

Because if I lose myself in this kiss, in this moment, maybe he'll forget the question he just asked. Maybe, if we're both distracted enough, we can forget about the outside world for a little while. And just be together like two normal people. Ones without screwed-up baggage and messed-up families that have to be perfect in every way.

Oh, wait. That's just my family.

He leans back, then, nibbling on my bottom lip a moment before creating space between us. "What?"

I lower my forehead to his, his beard soft beneath my palm. "You're too good to be true," I whisper. Because that is the single, most honest thing I've ever said to him.

"Everything has a catch," he says softly. There is darkness in those words, cloaked in mystery. I can't figure him out. This man who said no to me the first time I asked him to do dark and dirty things to me in a dark and dirty place.

His palm is warm on my cheek, comforting and sexy. Maybe now, maybe this time, he will finally touch me where I want him to touch me. Where I need him to touch me.

Maybe once, just once, he will slide his fingers over my skin, whispering words that make no sense, filling me with sensation that blocks out the things I need to forget.

"What's the catch with you?"

He shakes his head. "We're not talking about my secrets right now. We're talking about yours."

I smile thinly. "The only secret is what I want you to do to me."

He laughs. Not exactly the reaction I was going for. "That's no secret." His voice is low and deep. He's watching. Waiting. "I'm waiting." He brushes his lips over mine. "Trust me enough to talk to me."

A feral thing pretending to be civilized.

I want. I want to dig my fingers into those broad shoulders. I want to feel his powerful hips between my thighs. I want to pretend for one damn moment that I'm a normal person who gets to pick who she sleeps with and when and how often.

I'm denied even that.

I don't have the words to tell him about Davis. About my father. I can't push them from the place inside me that's lined with shame and give them life in the world.

Just like that, something cold washes over my skin, erasing the warmth from his touch. It's always about what other people want. Always about their needs. Their feelings. Their fucking campaigns and their reputations.

My lungs close off with sudden, frustrated anger.

"Never mind."

I'm on my feet and out the door before I think he knows what hit him.

Part of me hopes he'll follow me. Part of me hopes that he'll be that fantasy that stops my flight and begs me to stay.

I am disappointed. Yet again.

It's an odd feeling to be angry and disappointed and unbearably aroused.

Money. People kill for it. And yet in this moment, the only thing I want, money can't buy.

I'm not sure where I'm going. Just away.

Down the gentrified streets of Durham where the New South is pretending the sins of the Old South are long forgiven. Past the gluten-free bakeries and the trendy tea and coffee shops.

It's all bullshit. All of it. You can't erase the sins of the past by covering it up with a coat of paint. The memory of the blood in these streets is still there, captured in the stone.

"How long are you going to walk for?"

I keep walking, despite the tiny skip of my heart at the sound of his voice.

"Until I'm not angry anymore."

He falls into step beside me. "Going to be a while, then?"

He's not even breathing hard.

That pisses me off even more. I'm quite possibly being irrational. And I really don't care. "Probably."

He says nothing for about two blocks. Maybe more.

The sky is darkening overhead. Thunder rumbles in the distance.

"Storm coming in."

"You can head back. So you don't get wet."

"I've been caught in the rain before. Lots of times."

I start down a hill, the broken cobblestones shaded by an ancient tree. I don't want him here.

"I'm quitting when we get back to The Pint." The words are out before I really think about them. I can't do this. Not with him. Not anymore.

"Any particular reason?"

"Pick one."

He stops me then. Grips my upper arm and halts my rush to nowhere. "Why don't you start with telling me what set you off back there? I'm pretty good at reading people but I'm not a fucking mind reader."

I shake my head, the fury still a latent thing in my bloodstream. Dormant now, instead of pulsing, frustrated anger. "Why do you care? I'm just some unfuckable chick you hired out of some failed sense of obligation."

Something flashes in his eyes. Something dark. Something wild. Like the storm overhead.

He steps into my space. His fingers are hard on my jaw. "I don't ever want to hear those words come out of your mouth again."

My rebellion is fierce and not entirely thought out. I yank away before he finishes speaking. "You really don't get it, do you? You're giving me orders just like everyone else in my life, and I'm so damn tired of it." I back away, hoping my voice will stay steady for a moment longer. "I'm done. I'm so done with all of this."

My voice betrays me. Cracking as the sky above opens up and unleashes freezing hell over both of us.

I turn away, walking into the rain and the fog and the cold.

It's a small act.

But at least it's my choice.

Eli

I'M NOT the smartest guy in the world but as I watch her walk away, I can suddenly see the roadmap of every way I've fucked up since Parker walked into my life.

Refusing to do what she wanted. Demanding she open up when I've refused to do the same.

In that instant, I know everything about her. And it is achingly clear just how badly I've screwed *everything* up.

She needed me to be different. To let her take control. And instead, I did exactly the opposite.

My skin is cold and wet, matching the ice that fills my lungs with every breath.

I don't know how to fix this.

But I can't leave her alone. I can't let her walk away into the fog and the rain and hope she makes it home okay.

I catch up to her easily, falling into step next to her.

She says nothing. Her head is down, her hair pushed back off her face even as her shoulders are slumped against the downpour.

"I have this problem," I say after a moment. "I can't let people walk away mad." I swallow, not wanting to say the next words but knowing that she needs to hear them if she has a chance of ever seeing the real me. "Because I might not ever see them again."

She swipes her hand over her cheek, sliding her index finger beneath each eye.

"That's incredibly sad," she finally says.

It's also the most honest thing I've ever said to her. But I don't tell her that. "You asked me once why a bar. Why here?" I rub my hands over my beard, pushing my hair out of my face. "I was alone. I missed my tribe. My soldiers. My friends." I swallow. "I lived my entire adult life for one purpose: leading soldiers. And I didn't have that anymore."

"So you made your own tribe."

It's amazing how easy the words are right now. In the rain and the fog and the cold. The outside matches the inside, and the words have no barriers now to stop them. "Yeah. Deacon was the first. Then Noah and Josh. Kelsey."

"I like Kelsey."

"She doesn't trust easily. But she trusts us more than anyone else." I hesitate, not sure how much this talk of tribes and family made by war and not blood might alienate her. "She is as much a part of my tribe as any of the guys."

Parker keeps walking, her head down now, her movements less angry.

"I wish I knew what that feels like," she whispers, so quietly I almost can't hear her over the rain.

"What?"

"That kind of trust that has you hiring complete strangers based on a shared experience and nothing more."

I want to reach out. To pull her close and let her lean against me. To feel her body mold and shape against mine. "Most people don't."

"That's really a shame. That you have to be willing to kill someone in order to even come close to it."

Her words catch me off guard. She's right but that doesn't make her words any less sharp. "*Si vis pacem, para bellum.*"

She pauses then, looking up at me through the rain. "To secure peace, prepare for war."

I smile faintly. "I'm mildly impressed right now."

"Had to learn Latin in high school."

"Hell of a high school." I have a sudden fantasy of her in one of those prep school uniforms with the short skirt and knee-high socks and sweet baby Jesus I'm going to embarrass myself. "You don't agree with the sentiment."

"Which one? High school or war?"

"Either?"

She looks away then and starts walking. She hasn't been paying attention but I've been steering her back toward The Pint and relative warmth.

"I've never encountered a situation that calls for war."

I stop her then. Right there in the cold rain. I touch my thumb to the faint yellow around her upper arm, all but healed. "The man who did this to you is a coward." I brush the pad of my finger over her skin gently. "That's worth going to war over."

"Be that as it may, I still have to marry him."

Her words are an ice pick to my heart, but I keep my expression blank. This is the first time she's said anything about her life. I can't fuck it up again. "You have a choice."

She shakes her head. "I really don't." She turns her face to kiss the palm of my hand. "But it's nice to pretend for a while that I do."

I open my mouth. I want to argue with her. To tell her to fight back. To prepare for the war she needs to secure her freedom. But I don't.

Instead, I lift her face to mine, capturing her lips in a soft, warm, and wet kiss. She opens for me, her tongue touching mine in the sweetest caress. I could stand here forever, tasting her, living in the moment of just feeling her breath mingle with mine.

Her fingers twine into my hair, her nails dig into my scalp as she pulls me closer, taking what she needs. I am content just to be needed in that moment. The fire of her touch burns away the cold and the rain and the wet, leaving only the sensation of her skin against mine, her breath filling me.

She shivers against me, the tremble running through her body and into mine.

But neither of us moves, caught in the moment between sensations. Unable to break the connection and return to the real world where she is trapped in her past.

And I am trapped in mine.

CHAPTER 15

Eli

THERE IS fear in every beat of her heart beneath my fingers. Fear. Anger. Disappointment.

I saw all of those things flash before me the moment before she stalked out of my office. I've never followed a woman who walked away before.

I have no patience for games.

And it wasn't the fear or the anger or the disappointment that compelled me to go after her.

It was the courage that it took for her to stand up and walk away.

What pushed her to the breaking point? I only know I can't push her any further. Whatever she's running from, whatever she's trying to hide from, she's not ready to talk about it.

I can wait.

Lightning cracks overhead and I flinch, pulling her close. I half shield her with my body. "Storm's getting closer."

"You don't like them?" She looks up at me and I realize how well she fits against me.

"I don't mind them. When they're not right overhead." I stroke her cheek as the rain splatters on the back of my hand. It's a stark contrast to the warmth beneath my palm. "I have a place. Above the bar."

She makes a noise in her throat. "Of course you do."

I brush my lips against her mouth, the want inside me an ache that burns through my veins.

I don't remember the rush back to my loft. I remember taking her hand and guiding her through the huge splatters of rain that turned into a flat ass downpour a block from my stairwell. The thunder rolls through the sky as I close my door behind us, and then it hits me.

She is here. Completely soaked. Completely vulnerable.

Completely mine. Even if only for a night. An afternoon.

I wish I knew how long she'd stay. I wish I knew what to say or do to get her to trust me.

But she's here now.

And I cannot screw this up.

She shivers.

I step to her, drawing her mouth up to mine. It is a gentle kiss, meant to warm. To comfort. To sip from her.

I don't expect her to step into my space, to bridge the gap between us. She slips her hands beneath my shirt. Her palms burn my chilled skin.

"God but that feels good," I whisper against her lips. She frowns, and I kiss her brow. "Can I take your clothes?"

She smiles wryly. "That's pretty forward."

I nod at a small closet near my kitchen. "Dryer." I kiss her again. "I'll be honest. I want to see you." Her lips open beneath mine. "Taste you." I nip her bottom lip. "Every. Inch of you."

Her fingers curl into my sides. I cover one hand and urge her to slide it up, higher beneath my shirt, until her palm rests over my heart. "Touch me," I whisper.

It takes every ounce of willpower I have to stand there and let her fingers trace over my skin as she pushes my shirt over my head.

I know what she sees. Evidence of the war, etched and cut into my skin. She traces her index finger over the scar on my shoulder. The broken, burning piece of rebar would have effectively ended my Army career if I'd still had one when I'd gotten hurt.

She surprises me. Steps close enough to me that I can feel the heat from her body and presses her lips to the scar and the awful black ink I used to mask its terribleness.

"What don't you want to forget?"

I swallow hard and turn to her. "A lot of things."

I slip my index finger into the waist of her pants. "You're wet."

She grins. "You have no idea."

I laugh and tug her close, slipping her wrap off her shoulders in a single movement. It lands in a plop on the floor. I'll get it in a few minutes. In this moment, I want to focus on Parker. On learning what she needs and wants and likes.

I tug her back against me, wanting to feel the pressure of her body against mine. She's a perfect fit, everything molding into place like she was made for me. She tips her head, offering her flesh in an age-old sacrifice.

Her skin is cold beneath my lips. She shivers as I kiss her just where her collarbone disappears into her throat. She makes a noise as I trace the line of her shoulder with my tongue, pushing her tank off her shoulders. Her body is smooth lines and warm angles. I slide my thumbs down the line of her spine, still kissing her neck, suckling her a little as she shivers again.

I follow my thumbs with my tongue, tracing an erotic line down her back, pushing her pants down off her body. In part, I want to feel her against me, but my brain shut down the need to get her warm and dry, this need I have to protect her. To care for her.

She steps out of her wet clothes, and she is naked in front of me. She doesn't hide or cross her arms over her body. She is perfection, all soft bronze skin, dusky nipples and pale blond hair between her thighs. The want inside me is burning away all rational thought as she steps toward me once more.

"Tell me what you want." A whisper. One step short of begging her to let me touch her.

She slips one arm around my neck, rising on her tiptoes to press her body against mine.

But I'm in for a shock when her palm slips between us to cradle my erection and squeeze it gently. "Can I kiss you there?"

My eyes damn near roll back in my head.

Eli

SHE IS on her knees in front of me. It is the most erotic thing I've ever seen in my life.

There is trust in that simple gesture. I cup her chin, stroking my thumb over her bottom lip. I can't look away. Her lips part, and I slide the tip in, just a little. Her mouth is soft and warm and wet. She closes around the edge of my thumb, sucking gently, so gently.

I ache in a way I haven't ached in forever. This touch, this complete surrender to the feelings of erotic, sensual caress.

There is nothing about this that will end well. We are from two very different worlds. And no matter how much I pretend to walk in hers, I'm only visiting. Trying to get funding to keep my business open. Trying to make a difference.

Trying to pretend that the things I do still matter.

But this afternoon, when she walked away, I couldn't let her go. I looked in her eyes and saw something there that called to me. That made me need to make her believe that she was touchable. That she was worth more than the people in her life had led her to believe.

And now she is on her knees in front of me. Waiting, unsure about what to do next. My brain may want her some other way, but my dick is perfectly happy to oblige her at the moment with just how she is.

I have lost control of this situation.

But then she reaches for my jeans, her palm sliding over my cock. She squeezes me, still sucking gently on my thumb. She traces the tip of her tongue over the edge as she pulls my belt open. Jesus, I'm a fucking goner.

The air is cool on my stomach as she pushes open my jeans. I can't move even if I wanted to. I need to see this through. I need to do this right.

But I can't fucking move. I can't blink. I don't want to forget a single moment of the erotic image of Parker on her knees in front of me.

She slides my erection out of my jeans, stroking me gently. Christ, I'm hard as fucking rock. It's everything I can do not to guide her lips to me. To urge her to put that beautiful mouth around the tip of my cock.

I thought I didn't want this? I fucking lied.

She drags her teeth over the edge of my thumb a moment before she releases me. I have nowhere to put my hands now.

I drop them by my sides. I am not in control here.

"Can I kiss you here?" she whispers, rubbing her thumb over the aching crown.

"Yes please." The words are strangled. A plea. She has me under her complete control.

I am completely still as she moves closer. Rubs her lips over the tip. A soft, gentle caress. I'm ready to fucking beg.

And then she opens, tracing her tongue over the edge before sucking me gently, so gently into her mouth.

It's heaven. Pure fucking heaven. Her touch is electric, like a thousand points of heat with every slide of her lips over my cock.

I close my eyes and fight the urge to move, to rock into her.

This...this is supposed to be for her but it's not. Because I am a selfish bastard who is just like a thousand other guys who won't turn down a beautiful woman on her knees.

I'm no saint.

But goddamn, Parker feels good. Touching me. Licking me. Sucking me. I am lost in her touch. Lost in the complete and total need to let her control this, let her take this wherever it will go.

She sucks me a little harder. A groan escapes me. My balls tighten, and I can't fight the urge to rock into her. Just a little.

I reach for her then, urging her to let me go. To stand. And when she does, I pull her against me, harder than I probably should, and kiss her. I'm too far gone at the moment to do anything but kiss her. To drink from her. To take all of her inside me in that single gesture.

"I don't want to come like this," I whisper, nibbling on the edge of her meal.

"How then?"

"How do you want me?" A serious question. She needs to know that she's controlling things here. She gets to say how far we go. If we even finish. "Because right now? I'd sell the fucking bar to get you to agree to let me do terrible, forbidden things to your body."

"What are you waiting for?"

I smile and rock against her a little more. "Those five little words."

And then she is on my sofa, her upper body braced on her palms. I capture her face in my palms and kiss her gently, lowering her until she is supported. Slowly, sipping on her lips. Savoring the taste of her. "Can I touch you here?" I slide my fingers down over the length of one of her arms. She makes a noise. "Say yes," I whisper near her ear.

"Yes."

"Can I touch you here?" I trace my fingertips over the edge of her ribs, just along the swell of her breast.

Her response is a huff against my lips. I smile. "Say yes."

"Yes."

I brush the back of my knuckles over the tight edge of one nipple. A shiver runs through her.

"Can I touch you here?" A slip of my fingers against her inner thigh.

She makes a sound. A whimper. Maybe a plea.

"I need you to say yes." I manage to get the words out. Barely. They are somewhere between a whisper and growl. It takes everything I have to restrain myself but this...this isn't for me. "Please say yes."

I slip my finger a little closer, running it gently, barely there, over the seam of her body.

Waiting, intensely and painfully hard, for her response.

CHAPTER 16

Parker

HEAT BURNS across my skin the moment I clamp my thighs shut.

I knew where he was going the moment he carried me to the couch. But to feel his fingers dancing closer to the edge of my body...

He removes his hand, bracing himself on either side of me. His breathing is hard and ragged. He is partially between my thighs, partially covering me.

He leans in close, brushing his lips over my throat once more. The man is infinite patience. I want to drop to my knees in front of him and let him finish. To feel him let go and know that I wielded that power.

It'd be a small act of defiance in my caged little world.

"I love tasting you," I whisper. I close my eyes, unable to look at him as I admit what touching him with my mouth did to my insides. I drag my teeth over his earlobe. "When I pulled you into my mouth,

I imagined what it would feel like to have you push into me, to fill me." I breathe out the next words in a shame-filled rush. "That it wouldn't hurt. That for once, it would be like it's supposed to be."

He trembles and then stills, and there is silence between us. Nothing but the beating of his heart beneath my palm. The silence drags on so long, I'm not sure he's even still breathing. But for the warmth from his body, he might not be.

His expression is patient, but there's something more now. "So that night in the alley...it would have hurt you," he says, something close to anger lacing the edge of his words.

"Not so much. I'd had a couple of drinks."

He frowns then and shifts until his forearms are bent along my ribcage. He's kneeling on the floor. His mouth is a flat line. Disapproving. I know that expression all too well.

"Wait. Have you ever had sex sober?"

I shrug. "I was mostly sober that night."

"You didn't answer the question." Suddenly I feel guilty. Like I've done something wrong.

"Not since the first time."

He presses his lips together and looks away. Down at my body, where his hands are cradling my ribs. Finally, he glances back up at me, and I am poignantly aware of the raw power in the man that I've chosen to get naked with.

He leans close, pressing his body into mine. I can feel every hard line on his body, every hair pressing into my skin, making me into a reflection of him. Like a key pushing into a new mold, forming it to the outlines of its teeth.

Except that I will never be as powerful, as fierce. As independent.

I welcome the pain, the discomfort of him. I can feel him, hard and stiff against my thigh. Waiting. Patient, oh so patient. "So if I touch you..." He slides his fingers over the line of my thigh. "Here." Dancing against the edge of where I ache. I want the pain from his touch. I want his hands on me, no matter how much it will hurt.

I want to want something simple. And clean. And pure.

I want him. And I have since that first night.

He doesn't move for a long moment. Then, slowly, so slowly, he slides the tip of his finger over the seam of my body. I brace for it, for that slice of pain of dry skin running over dry skin.

Despair is a real thing, clasping at my throat, squeezing it gently shut with every shattered inhalation.

It doesn't hurt.

His finger slides over me again, and I can feel the moisture from my body slicking over his finger.

"Look at me," he whispers.

I'm helpless to obey. The intensity of his eyes burns me like a physical thing. "Tell me how this feels." His voice is a hushed whisper. Gravelly and rough.

He lifts one eyebrow when I remain silent. He shifts then, cradling me against him, urging my thighs further apart. "I want to do this right." His voice is rough in my ear. "Tell me what you like." And he slides his finger over me, again and again, driving me quietly insane.

He's guiding us backward until I feel him tugging me against him. I'm cradled against his chest, my back pressed to that hard wall of muscle. I'm surrounded. He drags his teeth over the back of my neck, his finger dancing at the edge of my body where I am swollen and aching.

Then he shifts, spreading his own legs and dragging mine open.

I am completely exposed. He turns my face, kissing me then, his fingers brushing against my belly. His beard is soft and rough at once, his lips warm, his breath hot on my throat.

"Are you okay?" His voice is deep, rumbling against my neck.

"Better than you know." I don't want to risk him leaving. He's barely moved, but I feel like he's completed me in some way, just skin to skin. Simple. Uncomplicated in ways that my life can never be.

He shifts then, urging one of my thighs to inch open, further, just a bit. "Close your eyes."

I frown. I want to memorize every aspect of his touch. Watch his fingers move over my skin. Savor the contrast between his black-lined skin and mine.

"Please?" His breath burns my skin.

I swallow.

And surrender.

Eli

THE IDEA THAT SEX HURTS…I'VE heard it before but it's never really registered as a thing that really happens unless people are doing things wrong. Or intentionally, but that's a whole different ball of whips and chains.

In Parker's case, I've judged her wrongly. Again.

I assumed that a woman as well put together as she is would have…I don't know, maybe a training pool boy or somebody who would show her the ropes.

She radiates confidence in everything she does. How could she possibly have not…I stop. Because to continue down that path is to move toward violence.

Not toward her. No, never her. But toward the man that hurt her. Repeatedly. From what I can figure, it's the man who bruised her.

Please let the gods put him in my path.

I ease her off me and shift until I'm lying between her thighs, one leg draped over my shoulder.

I wait until her eyes close before pressing my lips to her belly once more. I focus on the sensation of her skin touching mine. The softness. Her warmth. She smells like vanilla and oranges and rain.

I should put her clothes in the dryer but that would involve leaving, and I'm quite comfortable where I'm at, thank you very much.

Her body is a perfect fit; her ribs fill my palms. I've got to tread carefully. I need her to relax. To forget. And I need her to do it sober.

It would be easier if she had a glass of wine. Or a shot of whiskey. It would take the edge off. Let her find a release without the stress of being locked inside her head holding her back.

But then she'd never realize that it was possible for two lovers to connect in a way that doesn't hurt. That doesn't involve alcohol.

A connect based only on trust.

I trace one finger down the line of her ribs. Slowly trail up beneath the swell of her breasts. They're damn near perfection, her nipples tight and dusky. I circle one tip lightly enough that she's unsure if I've touched her. Her expressions are priceless. She's concentrating. Trying to figure out where our flesh will meet next.

I lick the tip of my finger, then trace her nipple again. A little firmer. Her breath hitches. She doesn't exhale. Waiting. Waiting.

I blow on her skin where it's moist, and she exhales with a rush, the air shivering from her lungs. She's tense beneath me.

I want her. All of her.

It's a powerful thing to be wanted. But I need her body to tell me that, not her mouth. I need to know, to feel it in her response.

I flick my tongue over her nipple then bite down sharply. She makes a noise deep in her throat, somewhere between a gasp and a cry. She wriggles a little and arches her back, opening her thighs a little more.

I can think of nothing better than settling down and feasting on her. I mean to be patient. To go slow. But when I look down, I can see her swelling, her body responding to the slightest stimulation.

Oh, how I want to believe she will come beneath my lips. That I can banish the terrible lover who has convinced her she doesn't deserve her own pleasure. That she's incapable of it.

Watching her body swell…it hits me, hard. That this…this isn't some cheap fuck in an alley.

I slide the tip of my index finger over the part of her clit that's peeking out from her folds. It's warm and soft and smooth and slick with her own heat. She makes another noise. Her thighs tighten around my body but she doesn't move. Doesn't open her eyes. I slide my finger over the seam of her body once more, savoring the delicate friction. Wanting to feel her body's wetness. Savoring the purity of the moment as she swells a little more beneath my fingertips.

A woman's body is a magical thing. I touch her, a little more firmly this time. Parting her folds, exposing her where she's fifty shades of untouched pink. I wait for her to open her eyes, to watch every movement I make.

Her eyes are on me as I open my mouth and gently touch her with my tongue. Just the tip. Just to see how she reacts.

And she comes almost completely off the couch. This time her hands fist in my hair as I touch her again, licking her with a hint more pressure. I'm torn between watching her body and watching her expressions as I touch her.

Her lips are parted, her face a relaxed mask of pleasure. Pure, simple pleasure. The way it should be between two consenting adults.

I hesitate, unsure if she can take it, then open my mouth over her completely, dragging my tongue hard over her swollen flesh and sucking her where she's pulsing and ripe.

A spike of something raw and powerful surges through me. I want…I want to push inside her. To draw this out for both of us.

To feel her spasm and clench around me until we both crash into the void.

But I don't. I focus on her pleasure. On every sigh, every spasm in her thighs. Using my tongue, my fingers, every trick I've learned from a thousand casual encounters to draw her out of her shell. Until she can't restrain herself. Until her thighs squeeze tight around me and her fingers thread into my hair, as much to anchor herself as to touch me.

She's there, right there. I take her hand, threading mine with hers. Guide her fingers to her own flesh, wet with her own moisture. Watch the surprise flash across her face as she realizes her body is so slick and ready.

And then she's gone, flying apart in my arms as I continue the sensual onslaught.

I watch her come apart beneath my touch, my tongue, and I am undone. I reach down, stroking myself as she comes, using her pleasure to finally reach my own. To shatter with her, even as she's gone away where I can no longer reach her. My own orgasm rips through me, sending a violent release spiking through my body.

It is only the beginning.

It is enough.

CHAPTER 17

Parker

REGRET IS A POWERFUL THING.

There are too many things in this life that I regret already.

Lying on the couch with Eli is not one of them.

No, my only regret is that I have to leave. I have to go and meet my father. Because if I don't, if I try to play games, I will lose.

Like always.

Frustration pushes aside the warmth in my body, replacing it with the chilled press of time draining my lungs. I'm not sure what the polite way is to tell a man who just did unimaginable things between your thighs that you have to go but, well, there I am.

I'm loathe to move. To breathe. Not when he's just done something magical and possibly illegal in several countries.

I want the need to disappear. But I don't want to forget this. The warmth of his touch, the heat of his body—he surrounds me for a moment and I simply am basking in the realization of what we just did and the fear that I may never, ever feel as good as I do in this exact moment.

His head is resting on my belly, one finger idly sliding over my skin. The caress in itself is something magical. Something beautiful in its simplicity. Who knew it was so nice just to be touched in such a familiar way?

I can feel the pressure of the clock against my lungs. It's impossible that he can't feel it, too; creeping into my muscles, tightening and tensing and pushing away the languid pleasure, but he seems oblivious.

He shifts, pressing his lips to my belly just below my navel, and then he rises, standing in a single, effortless motion.

He is naked.

His body is like nothing I have ever seen in a man before.

Broad and thick. Tattoos jitter down each of his arms and over each shoulder, until the black lines meld into the hair on his chest.

He is a warrior from another time. Completely foreign in my world of manicured men and perfectly sculpted haircuts. Whether they were born that way or not is irrelevant.

Eli is more than how nature intended him—he is what he made himself to be.

And it hurts—a raw, pulsing ache somewhere near my heart—that I have to walk away. Right now. Because if I don't meet my father, there will be hell to pay.

And the price…the price is too high.

I sit up and try to look away from the man standing in front of me. Away from the want, from the ache.

And then he extends his hand. A simple gesture that forces me to look up at him. At the confusion and worry that are churning like controlled chaos in his eyes.

I take his hand. Because I would be a coward not to.

He tugs and I slip into his arms. A gentle embrace, made erotic and intimate by the contact of our skin. He has said nothing.

Merely wraps me in his arms, as though he can feel the panic written in my veins.

It calms me to stand there breathing him in, letting the afterglow of his touch fight for supremacy over the growing pressure of time building in my chest. I can feel him tense beneath my palms, his back tight.

"I have to go," I whisper finally, breaking the silence between us. "I don't want to."

"Then don't." His voice rumbles beneath my ear.

I could lie to him. Tell him I have somewhere else to be than where I'm going. Telling him the truth would only lead to questions, an intrusion of my real life into the fantasy I've escaped into for the moment.

"I have to meet my father."

"You say that with all the joy of someone going into the hospital for an appendectomy. Without meds."

I laugh because his comment is unexpected and laced with an understanding that is oddly comforting. "Let's just say it's not an appointment I can miss."

The storm outside rumbles overhead, more distant now. "Unless by some act of God the storm prevented him from getting here."

"Sadly, my life doesn't work that way."

I can wish all day long that I could stay here, locked in this embrace with this man—our bodies pressed together, breathing in time, standing alone in space and silence.

He cups my cheek and urges me to look up at him. "You can't go anywhere until I dry your clothes." There is mischief in his eyes, a faint smile teasing around his lips.

Just like that, the panic that had been lingering expands, blooming into a wild, dark mold spreading inside my chest. I needed to be at the fundraiser. The consequences of not going... I'm not ready to face those.

"Hey." His fingers are strong and warm against the skin of my throat. There is concern in his eyes now. It's at odds with the sexual caress of his body against mine.

I don't move. Not to retrieve my still-wet clothing or to retreat from the lure of his touch. I want so badly to stay.

I brush my lips against his. "Thank you," I whisper. It's all I can manage at the moment.

He smiles and this time, it doesn't reach his eyes. "I'm not quite sure how to read the situation, to be honest. I kind of hope there's a real emergency you're rushing off to, otherwise..."

I laugh and bury my face against his chest. "There are no complaints on my end," I whisper. "You can bet your sweet, magical fingers that I'd be staying if I didn't have a really important thing to do this afternoon."

"That's good." He tips my face up. "Because we haven't even gotten to the good stuff yet," he murmurs before crushing me to him, claiming my mouth in a way that leaves me gasping. He slips his hand between us, his fingers skimming over the swell of my breast. My skin tightens, and I'm aching for him all over again.

"What's the good stuff?" I'm desperately clinging to the sexual pleasure in his touch. Avoiding the darkness stalking closer with every tick of the clock.

I half expect him to whisper filthy things.

Instead, he steps away, an evil smirk on his lips. "You'll have to wait and find out."

I throw a wet sock at him.

CHAPTER 18

Parker

MY DIRECTIVE IS ABSOLUTELY CLEAR. Be at the Turner House at exactly five thirty for introductions and cocktails with local big shots who need to have their egos stroked and to be reminded how grateful my father is for their continued support. His contracting company is one of the largest on the east coast. And having a future congressman as a son-in-law is guaranteed to make his life easier, despite nepotism laws.

Because that's how my father operates. He rewards loyalty so long as everyone remembers where they stand.

There are few things in life more awkward than meeting your father after you've just had the most mind-blowing afternoon in your entire life.

And yet, that's exactly what I'm doing. Rushing around my apartment like a madwoman. I need to shower and look presentable in less than an hour.

I've done it in less time before. But never with the burning distraction of Eli Winter running through my brain like a rabid and well-hung hamster.

Jesus, I can't believe what I said this morning. Of all the ways I'd imagined finally getting what I wanted, it never dawned on me that I was going to confess that sex hasn't exactly been an enjoyable experience for me.

And have him basically go, *yeah, challenge accepted.*

I smile as I step out of the shower and twist my hair up in a towel.

How on earth am I supposed to buy myself more time?

I'm not ready for my fantasy life to end. The one where I work in a bar where people actually give a shit about each other. Hell, where they actually know each other's names. That's nice in and of itself.

I pretty much manage to create a miracle by the time three o'clock rolls around.

I toss on a Brooks Brothers skirt and sweater with flats and do my makeup in record time.

I am presentable, which is how he will expect me to be. I'm not allowed to gain weight or appear without makeup, even if I'm working out. I must always be perfect.

Which is why my afternoon with Eli was so...extraordinary. No expectations. Nothing beyond what I wanted.

My phone vibrates, and my stomach tightens into knots. It's rare that I have that visceral of a reaction for a calendar reminder.

I also know that what I want is irrelevant at this point. I've got a few more weeks at most before he yanks me back under his authority. My little game will come to an inglorious end, and I will be reminded, under threat of painful humiliation, just whose daughter I am and what that means for the choices I make.

But every choice comes with a consequence, and my appearance at the posh Chapel Hill address is just another choice in the long line of decisions that I don't really get to make.

The old house sits at the end of a long drive, lined with vehicle high hedges. Tall white pillars surround the front porch and appear to hold up the world. It's something out of *Southern Charm* —new money pretending to be old money except that old money doesn't have to look like it's old money. It just is.

It's something I tried to explain to my roommate my freshman year. She'd been from some ridiculously small town in New Hampshire and she'd worn these oversized sweatshirts and flannel. She'd looked like some tragic refugee from the '90s Seattle scene, and I tried to bring her into the current decade by telling her that wealthy people did not dress like they didn't have any money. Those were hipsters, trying to be ironic.

We had a huge fight about her underwear, and well, the relationship never recovered.

This house is too much like Jaylee's underwear: trying too hard to be something it's not. You can't just ram cheap cotton up your ass and pretend you're wearing a thong. This house has too many flowers in the wrong places, too many replicas of famous paintings, as opposed to the famous paintings themselves.

I hand my keys to the valet and prepare to face my destiny. The one good thing that will come from tonight is that Davis won't be able to cause a scene in front of so many well-heeled donors. I'll pretend to be a good fiancée, and he'll pretend to be a good future husband, and the fiction that we are a model family will survive another day.

The floor beneath my heels is polished concrete covered in a Persian medallion rug of deep blue and ivory. It contrasts with the natural stone in a way that isn't, like the rest of the house, trying too hard.

I search for Davis or my father in the already filled room, wondering briefly what the price per plate of this event is. I'm guessing between five hundred and five thousand dollars. The current room is probably the five-hundred-dollar club. Davis is too smart to ignore the smaller donors for the larger ones.

"You look like you'd rather be French-kissing a water moccasin."

I turn at the sound of a familiar voice, not hiding my surprise at seeing Kelsey standing next to me, wearing a crisp button-down white blouse and fitted black slacks. Completely different from the tank top and jeans she wears at The Pint. "What are you doing here?"

"I'm working," she says mildly.

I narrow my eyes. "I'm confused. You have two jobs?"

She frowns at me even as she offers a drink to a passing woman wearing a ten-thousand-dollar diamond ring. "No. Eli's providing the alcohol service here."

All the blood leaves my face. "He's here?"

Kelsey turns away, toward a cluster of women I've never met before, but nods toward another room off to one side of the great room we're in. "Tending the bar. As always."

I follow the direction she's pointed toward.

And through the double French doors, I see him, standing behind the bar, smiling flirtatiously at a woman old enough to be his mother.

Oh, this whole thing just got really awkward in a sexually charged kind of way.

Eli

THE KIND of money at this place is the kind of money I need to keep my business both running and growing. The hostess, Kathleen, is a woman who could have walked straight off the set of *Real Housewives of Raleigh*, if there was such a show. She's wearing cropped white pants that hug her curves and a flowing light blue top that barely conceals whatever she isn't really trying too hard to hide.

I like Kathleen. She doesn't talk to me like I'm some kind of freak show. She's inspected my tattoos and definitely has given me the vibe that I could partake of her favors if I'm so inclined. It's flattering more than anything.

At least, that's what Deacon told me before he mentioned that he'd spent an afternoon with her, and it was quite possibly the most interesting afternoon he'd ever had.

Which for Deacon the Dark and Grumpy was saying something.

Someday, I'll get him to tell me just what was so interesting about that afternoon, but for now, I need to keep chatting her up to make sure that when I send the bill, it gets paid in a timely manner.

And since tonight's bill is starting at ten thousand dollars, I'm going to keep smiling until my face cracks. It's enough to have me taking out all the stops to make sure that Kathleen is exceptionally happy with our service tonight.

Which is why Deacon is also here. Their afternoon was friendly, so I'm sure having him around can't hurt. I hope.

The event tonight is some kind of political party fundraiser, and I've been directed to make the expensive whiskey the centerpiece of the night.

Easy enough. Except that I about had a heart attack transporting it: there's nothing like carting around a few thousand dollars in whiskey and praying you don't get into an accident.

The air is thick from the rain. It clings to my skin, drawing my clothes tight against my body in a way I haven't felt since Iraq. It's one of the reasons I prefer the modern conveniences of air conditioning.

But when people are hot, they drink. And when they drink...

A sliver of movement catches my eye, and my attention is

drawn to a woman dressed in an amber sweater and soft beige skirt and shimmering in the afternoon heat.

Parker. Her hair pinned up, revealing the arch of her neck, the smooth curve of her skin. I imagine her pulse against my lips right where her collarbone disappears into the scoop top fabric.

She is smiling, talking to Kelsey, who is playing the dutiful, polished waitress to absolute perfection.

I watch her for a moment, feeling like I've caught a glimpse into her unfiltered world. For a moment, she is smiling and open and poised. The Parker I remember from that day in my office when she was demanding I give her a job, all while making me feel like I was doing her a favor.

I feel like an idiot for not piecing things together. Of course this is where she was supposed to be tonight.

Apparently she's political royalty, because the man who's just appeared owns the room. He's a younger man but that does nothing to negate the power he has as he parts the crowd, sliding toward her. I watch as her smile falters just a little. Tightens at the edges.

I'd have never noticed if I hadn't been watching her.

But I've seen the unfettered smile she offers when she really relaxes.

And that is not it.

There is something like rage tight beneath my ribcage as Davis Harcourt, first-term congressman from Virginia, melts out of the crowd and walks toward Parker like he knows her. Which apparently, he does, because he grips her shoulders and leans in for a kiss that Parker deflects easily, leaning in to brush her cheek against his and pat his arm.

It's meant to be smooth. And it is.

Unless you're watching for it. Which I was.

Here is the source of her bruises.

What the hell kind of life does she have that she has to dodge a man's touch in public?

"Calm down." Kelsey's voice is a balm on my skin.

I turn my attention back to the whiskey I'm pretending to line up neatly on the stainless-steel cart. "I'm calm."

"You're about as calm as a long-tailed cat in a room full of rocking chairs."

"That's quite the turn of a phrase," I remark, trying to keep my voice light.

"It's a gift." She lifts one brow and pins me down. "Seriously. Stop glaring. You're the help. You don't get an opinion at events like this."

I swallow and consider my words carefully. "If my guess is right and Davis Harcourt is her fiancé, she's in for a world of hurt behind closed doors."

"You saw that, too?"

"In public, when she knows she has to have a hundred cameras on her, capturing every move." I look back over at Parker.

"Stop," Kelsey says mildly. "Get your smile on and practice being invisible. That's how you get invited back to events like these. They have to love you but not know you're there."

Kelsey is right but I can't stop watching Parker. Across the room, she appears in her groove. She's talking and smiling and blending in with all the right people. She doesn't laugh too loud. Doesn't do anything that isn't perfectly poised and planned.

It's like watching a facsimile of the Parker I've gotten to know. The Parker who says the first thing on her mind. The Parker who makes me laugh when I'm trying to seduce her.

No, that Parker is not in front of me. I have to wonder which one is real. Is the Parker I spent the early afternoon with who she really is? Or was she just playing me, determined to win at any cost? Because that Parker—*my* Parker—is not the woman I see across the room.

My Parker may not really exist.

She may have only been playing a part.

Just like I am tonight.

CHAPTER 19

Parker

THERE IS no way to avoid Davis. But I damn sure didn't have to antagonize him like I did.

Why didn't I just let him kiss me on the cheek? I should have. I saw the annoyance flicker in his eyes the moment I shifted away and brushed my lips against his cheek.

But the wave of revulsion I felt when he approached nearly undid my carefully done mask of perfection that I am expected to always present.

He doesn't like it when the people around him are less than flawless.

I know all too well the risk of being less than perfect when I'm around him. I won't do it again.

But the idea of him touching me...my skin physically recoiled from him, taking my body with it.

I didn't do it on purpose but that doesn't matter. Away from prying eyes and documenting cameras, I'm going to pay for this later.

For now, I'll play the dutiful fiancée.

The hostess, Kathleen, wants a picture of me with my father's third wife, Lainey. Oh the joy. She slips her arm around my waist, her smile as flawless as mine.

"Have you been hitting the bars? You've gained weight," she says through her smile.

The hate burns. But it does not shine through. "Lovely to see you, too. I see the cocaine is keeping you thin."

"You have such a terrible mouth on you. Your father's right. Davis needs to get you in line."

"I'm not really a fan of spanking." My smile could have cracked glass. "But you know, you do you."

The photographer moves off and we are alone, surrounded by a sea of people who want to ask Lainey about her latest charity project.

A charity that I'm ninety-nine percent positive is simply a feel-good cause that directs most of its money to operations—it's a scam, as far too many charities are these days.

I slip away from Lainey, surrendering the spotlight to a woman born to bask in it.

I suddenly very much want to dye my hair and move to Tahiti where I can live out my days as a beach bum.

"Was that as painful as it looked?"

I smile at the voice that slips over my skin like a caress. It is tempting, so tempting, to lean back into his body, to feel his chest support me, his arms fold around me.

But that's a foolish thing to dream and an even more foolish thing to do.

"You have no idea," I whisper. I can't turn to look at him. I need to keep up appearances so that no one will be the wiser. "I didn't know you were providing alcohol service at this."

"I didn't know this was where you had to be tonight." He smiles, and it's a professional facsimile of the warmth I'm used to from him. "I guess that makes us even?" He offers me a glass of whiskey, which I take, sliding my fingers against his. He lifts both brows and eyes the glass as I sniff it. "Do you know what you're doing with that?"

I look down at the whiskey. "Drinking it?"

"Have you ever had whiskey?"

"Nothing remarkable comes to mind."

"Don't drink that, then." He swaps the drink in my hand with a champagne flute filled with what looks like a mimosa. "This is better. Something you're familiar with."

I tip my glass toward him. "Thank you."

I want to stay there and talk to him. I want to watch him work. This is my new natural environment. I want to watch him in it. He doesn't move like he's uncomfortable.

He moves like a wild animal who has been caged and tamed and put on display, performing for its dinner.

I open my mouth to speak. To tell him about Davis, who is here tonight and who I have to talk to. And allow to put his hands on me. And pretend like it is all that I want in this world.

That I consent to being a toy for a spoiled, vindictive man.

I don't. But I also don't have a choice.

I tried once to escape and failed.

"Go," he says quietly. "I'm here." I look up at him sharply, meeting his intense grey eyes. "If you need me."

I swallow the burning need his simple declaration stokes to life inside me. That simple promise. One he's probably made to every stray that's come into his life, but right now it is everything to me. Everything I've ever wanted.

And everything I cannot have.

Because I am a doll for my fiancé's showcase. A trophy for a father who is incapable of loving me.

I am not allowed to be anything else.

I turn away, disappointment squeezing my lungs, pressing the oxygen from my blood.

I take a long sip of the drink and it burns a path down my throat. He's laced it with something. His eyes are dark and filled with something terrible. But his gaze is not directed at me.

And in that instance, I take comfort, a strange comfort in knowing he's here. Even though there is literally nothing he can do, his merely being present wraps around me like the softest cashmere.

I walk back into the crowd, mingling with my fiancé's donors and all the others eager to come into the orbit of one of the most powerful men in Washington.

I'm not ten feet from the bar when Davis strides back in from the patio, instantly the center of attention.

He is polished and pressed. Leather that has been made soft and supple by lotion and care.

His smile is blinding when he sees me, just as it's meant to be.

We each have our part to play. Him the up-and-coming junior congressman from Virginia, setting the stage for a national run in the next election. Me, his dutiful fiancée, finishing up my dream of business school before we make things official. When I'll be far too busy running his social calendar to have dreams and aspirations of my own.

His dreams will become mine.

And I will recall that these are very First World problems, and I will smile and order custom furniture from a craftsman in his district because it is good publicity and shows our connection with the working men and women.

The unbelievable sadness grips me as I turn my cheek and this time, let him kiss me. His grip on my upper arm is tighter than it needs to be, just like his smile and the coldness in his eyes tells me that my debt will be collected.

Tonight.

Eli

SHE'S TRAPPED. I'd recognize that look anywhere. I start to take a single step forward when Kelsey catches me watching Parker again and shakes her head once.

Kelsey's right. But I can't just walk away, leaving Parker on her own. I saw the strength in his fingers gripping her upper arm, the whiteness of bone through flesh.

Leaving her behind, leaving her alone…violates everything that I am.

But I'm also a realist. There's no winning tonight. Not here. Not in front of the crowd.

But that doesn't stop the need, the pressure, the feeling that I need to do *something*. It is an impatient feeling, growing and building inside me. A violence I haven't felt in a long, long time, wrestling with the civilized presentation of self that I show to the world.

Despite the beard and the tattoos, I blend into this place, but I won't if I let the darker angels of my nature fly free, as they very much want, toward the man who gripped her arm like he wanted to crush her bones.

I am trapped in an iron cage of norms and expectations where anything I do will likely make the situation worse.

The utter helplessness twists in a dark dance with the need to do violence to protect what is mine.

Because she is.

She's part of my world now. The small family I've built around The Pint.

But she's mine in a far more primitive way, too.

She just doesn't know it yet.

"You are going to get fired without pay if you don't keep that overly aggressive stalker alpha male bullshit you've got going under wraps," Kelsey says as she refills her drink tray once more. "Take a break. I'll run the whiskey bar for a while. You need to go somewhere else and calm down." Her palm on my forearm is soothing and cool. "Seriously. Step outside and cool off. Deacon and I've got this while the speech is going on."

The party attendees have all migrated back to a seated ballroom—yes the house is big enough to have its own ballroom. It's a bit larger than an Olympic swimming pool, and the entire crowd fits easily in the space.

I scan the attendees, looking for Parker. She's gone. How appropriate.

I take Kelsey's advice for once and step outside into the moist heat. The sun is hanging heavy over the trees, casting long shadows over the manicured lawn. It's moments like this that I wish I hadn't quit smoking. At least I'd have an excuse for being outside, away from all the people. When you don't smoke, people just think you're weird. Or antisocial. Or both.

A cobblestone path leads around the vast wraparound porch to a small grotto. The trickle of water over the fake stone is oddly soothing. Guess nature doesn't have to be real in order to remind us of just how small and insignificant we are in the grand scheme of things.

I scrub my hand over my beard, trying to figure a way out of my Parker problem. I was raised not to avoid trouble. That if something was wrong you fix it. You stand up to it.

You don't ignore it.

But I was also a company commander, and I learned the hard way that you have to pick your battles carefully. Even ones that seem like they are a redline that must never be crossed.

The world doesn't work that way. Principles and morality are fine until the bullets start flying.

"How long are you going to keep up the silent treatment?"

I frown and slip behind the stone chimney of the fire pit.

"I'm sorry, Davis. I just needed some space to...figure things out."

Parker doesn't sound like herself. She sounds forced, her voice strained. Higher pitched than I'm used to hearing. And more...insipid.

I will myself to disappear. And I listen.

"I'm not used to being ignored. You know I hate being ignored."

"I know. I'm sorry. I was just...so shocked when you grabbed me."

"You shouldn't have made me so angry." They are standing on the other side of a hedge. He cups her face. If I hadn't seen the bruises on her arm or heard the drastically different tone in her voice, I would mistake the gesture for genuine care.

But it's not. It's controlling. Letting her know just how vulnerable she really is.

Frustrated rage burns in my veins.

CHAPTER 20

Parker

I'M PLAYING my part as well as I can. I've forgotten some of my lines. The ones that reassure Davis and say I'm completely to blame. That I'll do better next time, and no, I never meant to embarrass him.

My soul shrivels with each word. I know it doesn't have to be like this. That there are good men out there who don't need to prove their power in everything they do.

Who are comfortable in their own skin.

Who know where to touch me to make my body sing.

I want to be with that man right now. More than anything.

"I'll be back in Virginia by the end of the summer for a couple of weeks," I say.

"When you finish slumming at that hole-in-the-wall bar?"

My skin goes cold, my blood thickens in my veins, grinding to a near halt. "I'm sorry?"

"You honestly think I wouldn't find out about your little side project? Why didn't you just take the internship at Carlisle Industries? Why is this executive management program so much more important to you than I am?"

Because I didn't want to see a sixty-year-old penis ever again. At least not until I'm closing in on sixty myself. But, miraculously, those words are not the ones that come out of my mouth. For once. "Because I wanted to make sure I'm prepared to assist you as your wife. The executive management program is elite. For only the best. Think about how that will sound every time I'm introduced with your name."

He smiles, his ego stroked for now. "But I miss you. And I want you to come away with me. It's nice that you're doing this but it's causing too much trouble."

"It's not trouble. I'm fine. The bar is safe. The people are good. I'll get my case study complete for my statement of purpose and I'll be on the beach with you in a few weeks."

"You don't make any sense sometimes. You don't actually have to prove anything to anyone. You're not supposed to be a CEO to be my wife." There's an edge to his voice. One that tells me just how close I'm walking to the danger zone. The one where he slices at me with his words and tells me he's sorry later.

Until he grabbed my arm last week, he's never actually hurt me before. At least not physically.

How my mother would be ashamed of my weakness.

I place my hand on his chest, fighting the urge not to recoil from touching him. I part my lips deliberately and look up at him the way I know drives him crazy. "Look. I'm just working at The Pint for a research project. I want to finish this out then I'll be home. Back where I belong."

"Yes but you're slumming. You're hanging around people who were too stupid to go to college and ran off to play Rambo in some stupid war. Violent people. They went to war, remember? How do you know none of them are going to snap and shoot the place up?"

I release the breath I'm holding. This is old territory for the congressman's son. He hates the idea of military service. Disdains everything about it and the people associated with it. His father never talks about what he did during the Vietnam years, but I strongly suspect it had to do with military exemption.

"That's an unfair stereotype of veterans and one that's not going to play well if you ever get recorded saying it."

He smirks. "Who's going to record me? Besides, the veteran voting block is getting smaller every passing year. Once the Vietnam vets start dying off, their political influence will pass." He strokes my cheek and I use everything I am to avoid pulling away. "Just be careful. You never know with those people."

"You know, I took a class on violence last semester. It was fascinating stuff."

"I don't care, Parker," he says coldly. "Veterans' issues are not part of my plank and they're never going to be."

I never thought anything of it—not the violence, not the veterans' issues, not the war. Until I took that class. Until I met Eli.

Now? Now Davis's attitude grates because he's talking about people I know. Real people who made real choices and live with the consequences.

I bite back what I want to say and smile pretty instead. "It's not like I'm going to enlist and head off to Ranger School," I say dryly. Because I want to defend Eli and his service. I want to defend Eli and the people he cares about. The people who have taken me in, despite me being nothing at all like them.

"That's not funny." His words are laced with a subtle threat. Hard to believe that I'd thought him so sexy and exciting when I first met him.

"Sorry," I mumble. "Look, let me finish my project and I'll be home for a few weeks when we can talk about the wedding."

"Which, by the way, we're setting a date for. No more stalling while you go off to find yourself. You can find yourself at our house in the Hamptons where you belong. I've had to hire a catering company all summer because you're not there to handle things."

Oh, the humanity. That might be the first thing I think. Not what I say, mind you, because that would ignite the situation far beyond what I'm capable of handling at the moment. "I'm so sorry. I'm sure *In The Garden*'s owners are thrilled with your business, though. And that will help them write the donor checks at this winter's gala, won't it?"

He smiles now and it's the warm, self-assured smile I'd once mistaken as making him look handsome. "Very true." He leans in and kisses me gently. I have to remind myself to part my lips a little and make the right sound. A sigh that doesn't even remotely resemble the silent scream in my head.

"I'm going to go find your father and try out the whiskey bar. I hear it's quite well stocked."

I brush my hair out of my face and fight the urge to swipe my hand across my mouth. I want the taste of him gone. But I can't. Must play along. "The owner is creating quite a lot of buzz around here with his whiskey collection."

"I'm sure he is." And then he's gone, taking the scent of over-cologned man with him. The air is at once fresh and clean and I breathe deeply, savoring the feeling of filling my lungs until they threaten to burst.

Then I sink onto a stone bench. It's cold and rough on my thighs, penetrating the thin fabric of my skirt. "What the hell am I going to do?" I whisper to the universe.

I press my forehead into my hand and close my eyes, replaying the exchange for any possible errors or mistakes.

I have to get back inside. My father will be looking for me, and I'm expected to be present and smiling and pretty.

Something like dread curls in my stomach. I hate this part of my life. More and more every day.

"Want to tell me what the hell is going on?"

Dread in my belly curdles and turns sour at the sound of Eli's voice.

No. Not just his voice. The rage in his voice. The pure violence, constrained only by convention and politeness. This is so different than the danger I'm used to from Davis. There it's cold and calculating. Manipulating every sentence, every word, to make sure he gets what he wants.

In Eli, there is merely violence. Maybe betrayal.

Or hurt.

Maybe all of the above.

I inhale deeply. Breathe out again, just as controlled.

Then I summon every ounce of acting skills I've honed in a thousand interactions with powerful men.

And hope it's enough to convince him...of what? That I can stay? That I have power over my life that I don't really have? Or that everything I just said to Davis was a lie?

I wish it was. But it wasn't. It was the cold, hard, ugly truth.

I'm using Eli for a temporary reprieve from the prison that is my life.

And it's better for both of us if he just lets me go.

Eli

"Is this the part where you tell me I'm fired for being a deceitful, conniving whore, and I live with the regret of what might have been for the rest of my life?"

She's tense and the quip falls flat.

She's scared. I can see that in the tight lines of her neck and the flat press of her mouth.

I stay silent. There are no words for what I need to express right now. I want to tear down the entire fucking structure surrounding her, to blast the doors off the gilded cage and set her free.

My silence is destroying her. And yet the words I need are locked inside me, lodged in my chest.

She glances back toward the building. I hate the fear that flashes in her eyes. "I don't do well with long sullen silences. Could you say something?" She swallows the rest of her drink. It dawns on me that it's the same drink I handed her over an hour and a half ago. "I mean, how hard is it to say fuck off and die?"

If I wasn't so violently angry, I'd laugh. Her comment diffuses my anger. Just a little.

"This isn't the part where I call you names." I take a single step forward. "It's the part where you tell me what the fuck is going on. Why are you lying to your fiancé?"

I sink down onto the bench next to her as all the color fades from her face. "I'm confused." Her voice cracks over the words, like shattered glass skidding across a tile floor.

"I heard you. I heard what you said to him." I dare to cup her face, to urge her to look at me. "It wasn't you. It was your voice and your words, but it wasn't you."

She smiles sadly and shakes her head. "Yeah, it was." She looks away. "And it was all true."

Her words are a knife, slipping between my ribs and piercing my faith in humanity. "You're not a very good liar."

She scoffs quietly. "Yeah, actually I am." The bleak sadness in her eyes nearly breaks me. "You learn really quick growing up around men like my father how to tell the most convincing lies." She inhales sharply. "I have to go back in." She stands and the skirt shimmers down her body. It clings to her curves in all the right places and makes me wish we were alone so I could explore her skin and distract her from the fear and pain I see looking back at me.

"You have a choice," I whisper.

She shakes her head. "No, I really don't."

She walks away, her hips swaying gently in the skirt, her shoes clicking on the stone.

She was lying, even as she tried to convince me she was telling the truth.

I sit there for a moment longer, pulling all of my storming emotions back into the box where they belong, so I can function for the rest of the evening. So I can not throat punch this motherfucker and end up in jail.

As much as I bitch and complain every time Noah or Josh gets in a fight in the bar, I'd never hear the end of it if Deacon had to bail my sorry ass out.

I let her go. The very act of standing still corrupts something I thought was already black and broken, but apparently, I had farther to fall.

This night needs to end.

But instead of losing myself in inventories and end-of-month statements, I'm now smiling and making small talk with the wives about their favorite charities, at least one of whom wants to take my mind off my current woes. The woman chatting me up over a glass of Johnny Walker Black has to be twenty years older than me if she's a day. Her body is cloaked in a clingy white sheath dress that accents her curves. She's a stunning woman by any measure.

I'm not interested, but I smile and listen to her talk about her charity work, raising money for the local magnet school for gifted kids. It's supposed to be egalitarian, drawing the best kids from the state. But it's not. It never is. They let in just enough poor and minority kids to look diverse.

God, when did I become such a cynic?

Kelsey strolls back up and hands me a business card. "Bennington Hauser is in the green room, and he wants to meet you. He's throwing an impromptu dinner party Tuesday night and he wants to know if you can provide the drink service." She's looking at me expectantly. "I already told him you could do it."

"How do you know I'm not booked already?"

"Checked with Deacon." She tucks the card in my shirt pocket and pats my chest. "According to Deacon, Bennington Hauser likes to run thirty-thousand-dollar bar tabs."

My throat closes off at the dollar amount. "How much have we run up tonight?"

"We're closing in on fifteen. And the cost of alcohol—even the private label—isn't anywhere near that much."

I scrub my hand over my beard. Jesus that's a lot of fucking money for two nights' work. I want to say no, to not support the man who's putting Parker in this situation with her fiancé.

But then it dawns on me that I'd be able to keep an eye on things. An eye on her.

To provide cover and maybe a little moral support as she navigates a world I left willingly when I walked away from the gilded parties of the D.C. officer corps. Not the everyday officer corps. No, the rank and file were just like everyone else.

But I'd been different. Granted access to the top, if only I'd wanted to play the game.

And I'd wanted to. I'd wanted to see how it felt to command a battalion. To maneuver tank companies across the desert in formation.

That was over now. My aspirations, my moral compass, all ground to dust in the dried blood of a desert war my brothers are still fighting.

It takes money to have principles. And I want to keep my bar open. To keep my group of misfit toys together as long as I can.

I can do this. At least for a little while.

And I'll keep telling myself that it's all for a cause.

Even if that cause is a woman.

That I am lying to myself about, even now.

CHAPTER 21

Parker

I'M IGNORING MY PHONE. **Again.**

I've never contemplated murder, but I'm seriously considering it if Davis doesn't back off.

How am I going to survive being married to him? Maybe this is why so many of my friends' moms use prescription drugs. And wow, that's a hell of a life to look forward to.

Maybe if I wasn't such a coward, I could have broken free when I first tried.

The bar is empty, which is to be expected at ten in the morning. Light pierces the dark hallway that leads to Eli's office. After last night, I'm not sure why I'm hesitating but I am.

Last night, I'd been on the edge, perched precariously near the abyss of my future with Davis. Last night, I'd wanted to leap into the darkness, to fly away from all of it. To simply be in the darkness and alone. Free to make my own decisions.

This morning, all that felt melodramatic. Maybe it was, maybe it wasn't, but it certainly felt like a completely different person had walked away from Eli last night than the one who was walking toward him this morning.

Eli is deeply focused on his computer. His fingers are flying over the keyboard. Something dark and pounding is playing in the background. His desk is chaos, covered in papers and sticky notes and scattered pens. Behind him, a board with push pins and more sticky notes.

It's like a disorganization bomb went off in his office. Such a stark difference from the first time I was in here.

"How on earth can you concentrate in all this?"

He looks over the moment I speak. The concentration on his face is shattered, and his eyes flicker for a moment before shuttering closed. "It's actually driving me crazy. My OCD has been pinging all day."

I lean against the door. "You don't strike me as the kind of guy to make sure his socks are all folded the exact same way."

He folds his arms over his chest and rocks back in his chair. "It's not the same for everyone. Just like a lot of things." His eyes are boring into me, intense and inscrutable. "How did the rest of your evening go?"

There's an edge to his voice now. A latent energy just below the surface. "It was fine. I left a few minutes after I talked to you."

"And your stalker?"

"If by stalker you mean fiancé, he left me alone. He was more focused on meeting my father's partners for potential campaign donations."

His lips press into a flat line. There is caution in his eyes now. "So what are you doing with me? Because I assume this engagement didn't happen last night."

I have to look away. "I don't suppose there's a right answer to that question, is there?" My voice is steady. Barely.

"Depends."

"On?"

"Whether you're willing to be honest."

I look back at him now. "I've never lied to you."

"I didn't specify who you had to be honest with." His voice is smooth and steady. Way cooler than I feel at the moment.

I nudge my toe against the edge of the door that separates the hallway from his office. The floor is polished concrete. Style and function mixed into the perfect design.

"What do you want from me?" The words rip free, tearing at my throat despite their almost whispered tone.

He pushes back from the desk, the veins in his neck pulsing against his skin. "I want you to be honest with yourself. I want to know why you're staying trapped in a life that you clearly want to escape. I want to know what made you this intoxicating mix of fearless and terrified."

His words slice at me, cutting me in a thousand tiny nicks. No slashing. No burning. Just soft flaying of the shield around my very concept of self.

"It's not simple." I finally look up at him. "It never is for people like me."

"It's not the 1950s anymore. You have your own money, your own degree. You're not some piece of property to be traded for more land and cows." Frustration now. I can hear it lacing his words.

"You don't understand."

"Then make me. Tell me what the fuck is going on. Because right now, you want me to believe you have no choice, and I just can't fucking swallow that pill. You don't have to let him hurt you."

"Where am I going to go? Everywhere I go, people recognize me. I'm not one of the Kardashians, but a powerful defense contractor's daughter doesn't get to just let her hair down and do what she wants. If I break things off with him, he will cause a scene. And that will detract from my father's carefully constructed business campaign."

"Who gives a fuck about your father's business? I'm talking

about you." He shakes his head slowly. "The consequences for your decision are one day in the news cycle at worst. The most you'll get is a ticker below the latest bombing in Syria."

His response sets something off inside me. Maybe it's defense. Maybe it's the need to justify my decisions. The anger unfurls easily in my belly, like a pot that suddenly reaches its boiling point. "You don't get to tell me that the risks aren't that much. You've never been in the world I live in. You have no idea the power that my father wields and how many people would love nothing more than to drag him into a scandal."

He says nothing for a long moment. The silence drags on, spreading through the room and wrapping around me like a layer of regret. "Maybe I'll come back later." I turn to go.

Of course, he stops me in a way that is one hundred percent Eli.

"I'm afraid of heights."

I frown and turn back. "Now there's a non-sequitur."

"When I was a cadet, they sent me to Airborne School at Fort Benning. When you drive onto post, you see these massive airborne towers. My first day there, they're hitching kids to wire harnesses and dragging them two hundred and fifty feet into the air."

I'm intrigued enough to turn fully back and listen to this glimpse of his life before the bar.

"I was fucking terrified. I thought there's no way I'm going up that fucking tower and falling back to earth with a little piece of canvas that you hope breaks your fall." He stands and circles the desk, approaching like a panther stalking his prey. He is standing in my space now, his body close enough that I can feel the heat from his skin radiating into mine. His mouth is there, just there.

He lets the story hang there, unfinished and rough, his palm sliding down to cradle my throat. One thumb presses on my pulse. If he were Davis, his touch would inspire fear, not heat. But with Eli, every touch makes me feel alive. Burning.

I'm tense, waiting. Afraid this is some kind of game. Afraid that he will walk away again and I'll be left alone, with nothing but the shattered remains of my pride.

He nuzzles my cheek, making a warm sound in his throat. His beard is scratchy today, not soft. I feel every prickle along my skin.

"It's funny. You think you're going to die during the fall. That your heart will stop, and you'll be dead before you hit the ground." He reaches for me then, his palm rough and hot on my cheek.

He brushes his lips against mine. Need unfurls low and hot in my belly.

"But after you fall, you realize there was nothing to be afraid of after all."

Eli

I'M STILL angry with her. With her boyfriend/fiancé/whatever the hell he is. I'm angry at the man who raised her to think she's nothing more than a prop on someone's arm.

But in this moment, seeing her on the edge of despair, I can't push her any harder. She's not one of my soldiers. She hasn't been to war. Hasn't seen the world through the eyes of someone who has.

I know obstacles. And what she's facing isn't impassible.

But to her they are. They are deeply rooted at the core of who she is. Where did that fear come from? How can that uncertainty be mixed beneath the backbone I see on a daily basis in my bar and in my arms?

For her, the consequences of her decisions are life and death. I have to respect how she sees things. I can't force her to see it my way. No matter how much I want to rail at her to break free.

She can.

She just doesn't know it yet.

I have to wait. And I hate waiting. I hate being strategic and feeling like I'm manipulating the situation.

I haven't felt this level of helplessness since Iraq. Since that night when I found out what the men in my formation were capable of.

It was the stuff of nightmares.

It was the stuff that ended careers.

I didn't have to walk away. But I did. Because the decisions I made and failed to make led up to that day.

I hate that these memories keep circling. That I can't disconnect from them.

This feels like the same helplessness. Parker shivers beneath my touch. I want to rail at her. I want to tell her she can leave, that she can jump, that I'll be there to catch her.

But she doesn't believe. She doesn't trust. I wonder if she's ever had anyone in her life she could count on.

I want to drag her into my lap and let her hands explore my body. Feel her fingers trace the scars and the ink and the blood and the bone. I want her hands on my body, her tight little body to sink over mine and take me into her.

I know, I just fucking *know*, that if she has someone to run to, she'll take the leap. And even if I'm just a temporary landing, I'm okay with that. It would be enough knowing she was safe.

It's torture thinking of her going back to him. To not know if she's safe. Because she's clearly not.

He'll hurt her again. Because that's the way men like him are built. They're weak. They need power.

I don't move away. Don't give her space to breathe, to run. I'm daring her to touch me. Daring her to reach out and take the leap.

"I've never jumped out of a plane before. Seems like a foolish thing."

"It's the most terrifying fun you'll ever have."

She lifts her chin, just a little. "There are much more mundane acts that could be called terrifying."

"Such as touching me?" My patience is razor thin. I want to pull her away from the edge where she is close, so close to running away.

"It takes more courage than you know to keep my hands to myself," she whispers.

"Why?"

Her throat moves as she swallows. The action is entrancing, drawing me closer. "Because I can't. Things are different now."

"You were perfectly willing to fuck me the first night I met you. Nothing has changed."

Her lips press into a flat line. "Everything has changed."

"Why?"

She lifts her palm and slides it over my heart. The heat from her touch penetrates the thin material of my t-shirt, burning me. I want her hands on my body, her fingers digging into my skin.

She finally lifts her face and looks at me. "You wouldn't be some mindless fuck that I can forget." She swallows again. "I have to forget. I have to go back." Her fingers curl into my heart. "I have to let all of this go. And that's going to be hard enough already."

"What is this power that they have over you that you can't control your own life?" I cover her hand with mine. I can feel all the bones beneath her skin. Her fragility. Her strength.

"It's different for me."

"Everyone thinks it's different for them. It's not. You just have to take the leap."

"Leap to what?"

I'm not prepared for the challenge in her words. The dare.

The words lodge in my throat, rising faster than I'm prepared to admit.

I stand there, mute, tension winding through my veins, tightening until my skin feels too small for my bones. I can feel it, just beneath my feet.

I cup her face then with both hands. She is soft and warm and infinitely strong.

"Me," I whisper before I capture her mouth.

There is no restraint in my kiss. There is only need, raw and hungry. I need her to know the truth of what I feel. The strength and the promise of everything that could be.

I take the leap, leaning into her, drawing her close until her body is flush with mine. Her softness fits to mine perfectly. Like every other woman was just practice for the perfection that Parker is in my arms.

My name is a gasp on her lips. A prayer before she buries her face in my neck. Her hair is soft on my fists, a golden mass tangled in my fingers, her breath hot on my skin.

She makes the tiniest of movements. A thousand beats of her heart pound into mine. The feel of her breath absorbing into me.

For a moment, I simply hold her. Allow her to hold me. To lean as long as she wants.

She moves, then, her body arching into mine. A subtle touch. A hint of movement. But it's enough.

My hands slide down her back, cupping her ass and drawing her up, until her thighs circle my hips and her feet lock behind my back. Until she is pressed against the wall, her body flush with mine.

Until I can't tell where she begins and I end.

Until I am lost in the fall.

And Parker is tumbling with me.

CHAPTER 22

Parker

IT'S SO easy to lose myself with him. So easy to shut the world out and pretend this is a lifetime, not a moment.

With Eli, every moment is forever. A dark, sensual touch of pleasure.

I surrender as much as I am able. Drowning in his kiss, his taste—the hard, rough feel of his body against mine. I want to feel his skin against me. I want to drop to my knees in front of him and taste him again. To feel him tense and tighten beneath my lips.

I want to forget.

I cradle his cheeks, the wall holding me up, pushing me closer to him. "Can we go upstairs?" I'm impressed I'm able to talk.

He lowers his forehead to mine. "A better man would ask if you're sure." He nips my bottom lip. "I'm not going to ask if you're sure. If you come upstairs with me, I'll give you what you wanted that first night."

I smile then. "Took you long enough."

He makes a sound that could be a growl, could be a groan. I'm not sure and I'm not sure I care.

We are upstairs before I can blink. The apartment is Spartan and small. Functional. It smells like him. Like whiskey and spice and something crisp and clean.

It's funny that I didn't notice that the first time I was here.

I was distracted then in a way I'm not now. Every sense is heightened. Tuned into the scent, the color. The very feel of the man behind me, surrounding me.

Consuming me.

My blood is burning. I want to fold over in front of him and feel him slide between my thighs, fill me with that delicious pain.

I lean back, lifting my arms over my head, offering myself to his touch. My breasts are tight and full and I want nothing more than to crawl into his lap and let his hands wander over my skin.

His hands slide over my ribs, circling gently, just below the swell of my breasts. God but I want his hands on me. He nips my ear, his breath scorching a shiver down my spine.

"You've never had whiskey, right?" His words are liquid amber on my skin, flowing into me like a hot caress.

I shake my head, not wanting this moment to end.

My cheeks flame hot, like this is something to be ashamed of. "No."

"But you knew about all the brands in the basement."

"Just because I know about them doesn't mean I've tasted them." I try not to sound defensive. I'm cold now, the glow from his touch fading a little.

He turns me in his arms, a faint smile on his lips. "We have to fix that."

"Right now?"

"No time like the present." He laughs softly and pulls a cardboard tube off the top of his refrigerator. Laphroaig 10 year. I recognize the black and white label, the smooth green glass shielding the whiskey from the light.

He pours two small glasses, barely a finger's worth of the dark amber liquid. "I learned this on my first trip to Scotland. I was on R&R from my first tour in Iraq."

"You didn't go home?"

"No real reason to go home after a while." He looks up at me. "My father and I are like oil and fire. It's better if we don't spend any time together."

"That's...unexpected." I'm not sure how to process his revelation. "You're on your own then?"

He shakes his head. "I've got the bar. The guys."

"Your tribe."

He nods once, a silent acknowledgment of his life and his choice. "You pour a tiny drop of water in the whiskey to bring all the flavors out."

I make a face. I'm not overly excited about trying this, especially not right now when I really just want him to stop teasing me with promises of his cock that he never delivers.

I'm not a really big drinker, but I want so badly this man's hands on my body, that if this is a detour on the way to that destination, I'll try it.

"So this one is made in barrels smoked with peat. It's the smokiest whiskey I've ever tasted."

I frown. "Why would you want to drink smoke?"

"Life is all about the simple pleasures. Taste. Touch. You can't buy sensations." He hands me the glass. "Taste it. Don't shoot it."

I sniff the glass, hesitant, then take a brave sip. I've heard the stories of whiskey burning all the way down, but this is literal fire burning down my throat.

I cough and try to keep a straight face. I fail and he laughs. "Oh my god, that is literally like drinking liquid smoke."

"Not a fan?"

"Why would anyone want to do this for fun?"

He's still smiling. There is something vulnerable in that smile. Something warm and genuine that I rarely see in Eli when he's at work. There's a tension that's always there, but right now, when it's just him and just me, there's something else. Something I want more of.

"It's about the process. The time that it takes to perfect the drink. The time that it takes for all the flavors to fully release."

"It…definitely has a taste." The words get stuck in my throat. He is watching me. Like he did that first night I met him and he turned down carefree, guilt-free sex. "What?" A hoarse whisper.

He hesitates, dragging his hand through his hair. The tattoo on his upper arm flexes as he moves.

"I…I want to know what it tastes like on you."

My belly tightens instantly, a sharp bolt of heat straight to parts of my anatomy that are definitely doing the thinking right about now. Maybe not thinking. More like purring. Yes, parts of me are definitely purring.

His voice is deep and smooth and he's there, just there. He moves easily, straightening and coming to stand between my thighs, nudging them apart just so. His hands are braced on either side of my hips.

"I think this is sexual harassment of your employees," I whisper.

"So you don't want me to kiss you?"

He nips my bottom lip. The movement is at once hesitant and bold. He is a mix of contradictions. Powerful and yet, when he touches me, he's infinitely gentle. I would never have thought it. Not for a man who looks like him. "Where on earth would you get that idea?"

He is close, so close. I love the lines beneath his eyes, the softness of his lips beneath the harsh edge of his beard.

He brushes his top lip against mine. I can taste the smoke on his breath, doubling the residual flavor from my own drink.

His breath is hot on my ear, his voice vibrating against my skin. The air buzzes with energy, crackling and tight and tense.

He's close enough that I have to lift my hands. They curl into the solid wall of his chest. I can feel his heartbeat racing beneath my palm.

"I'm afraid."

"It's too late for that." His words are rough now. A tremble of restrained violence beneath my fingers.

I swallow hard.

"Parker?"

"Hmmm?" I don't want to think. I want to close my eyes and lose myself in the texture of his touch, his kiss. The way my stomach tightens when he looks in my direction.

"Can I taste you?"

Eli

I'VE NEVER BEEN SO to the point before with any woman and in that moment of her response, I am infinitely grateful that she is here and she is fearless, even as she's afraid.

Her confession from the other day burns me. Sex hurts her. And I refuse to be a source of pain for her.

The whiskey is a gamble. I don't want her drunk. I want her to know who is touching her, making her feel.

Making her come against my lips, my fingers.

I slip my thumb over her bottom lip, nudging her open. Her lips are moist. Soft. She flicks her tongue against the tip of my thumb, a slight smile on the edge of her mouth.

I want her open. Begging. I want her so fucking ready and wet that when I push inside her, she feels nothing but pleasure.

The thought of her tight body squeezing my cock is enough to drop me to my knees, to worship at the altar of her body.

Instead, I press my lips to the side of her throat where her pulse scatters. She is liquid heat, smoky and sultry.

Her body is waiting and eager. I brush my finger lightly over her nipple. "You're not wearing a bra." I don't bother to conceal the amazement in my voice. I'd been so distracted by her that I hadn't even noticed.

I'm a fucking blind man when it comes to Parker.

"Maybe I was hoping to drive you to enough sexual frustration that you'd finally have your way with me."

I laugh against her neck, then squeeze gently, flicking my thumb over the tight peak. "I think we've got to work on your strategy."

"Seems to be working pretty well right now." She spreads her thighs a little more. A subtle shift but I notice. Lust rockets through my veins. I want this woman in a primitive way. I want her bent over, her pink flesh exposed to only me. I want to suck on her until she screams my name.

I want to feel her coming around my cock.

I pinch her lightly and she makes a rough noise, deep in her throat. "Tell me if you don't like something." I nip her earlobe. "Tell me what you like."

She makes that noise again, driving me a little crazier each time.

I tug the edge of her leggings, thanking whatever gods may be for this brilliant fashion trend, and draw them gently over her hips. Her body glistens as I lean in and press a kiss to the top of her pubic bone.

"Up." I shift her until she's sitting on the counter, her pink and wet body perfect height for me when I kneel in front of her.

Her glass of whiskey is within reach. Watching her the entire time, I tip the glass, dribbling a little on the soft mound of her pussy. Her eyes never leave mine as I catch it with my tongue, before it runs into her slick folds.

I do it again, running it closer to where she aches, each time denying her the feel of my lips on her swollen, pink body.

Finally, I dribble a little where she is infinitely soft and wet. The direct contact shocks her and she jerks, trying to close her thighs. I capture her then, my hands holding her open, my mouth claiming the smoky whiskey and potent slick sweetness of her body. I suck her, watching her head drop back, her eyes finally flicker closed.

I lick her again, my tongue tracing her folds, learning what makes her hips twist, what makes her moan.

When I slip a finger inside her, she is pulsing and hot, right there at the edge of an orgasm. Right on the edge of falling.

As much as I want to be inside her when she comes, I want her mindless when I finally am. I want her flying high from the pleasure.

I want to ride it with her.

Her body tightens around my finger, clenching in wave after shuddering wave. There's something beautiful about this woman in her arousal. Like she's learning what she likes even as she surrenders to the moment.

I suck her hard into my mouth again, stroking her with my fingers, my tongue. My hips rock in time with the slide of my finger. Her body tenses again, twisting, her breath coming in tiny pulsing gasps. I stroke her clit with my thumb, slipping through the mix of whiskey and her own wetness, pinching her gently.

And then she's gone, flying, biting her lips together to keep from crying out. Even in this she attempts restraint, attempts control. I pinch her gently, and she comes unglued with a shout, her thighs locking around my shoulders. I hold my mouth to her, sucking her, licking her, driving the wave longer for her. Just her.

And then I'm there, waiting at the entrance of her slick heat. She's still gone, flying, her body trembling as wave after wave crashes through her. I kiss her, deep and slow, licking her lips, her mouth, drawing her back into me.

Praying that she's ready.

I press against her, just a little, a tormented movement in near-absolute stillness.

Her eyes fly open, her lips parted in a gasp. "Does it hurt?" I need her to know she can stop this. That no matter how much I want to push inside her, I'll stop.

She's holding her breath, her arms braced behind her. She's still, watching, her eyes drifting from mine down to where our bodies are barely joined and back again.

Her mouth moves, a single word a rush of breath. "More."

I can die happy. Knowing she's wet and ready, knowing I brought her to this…it's such a simple, powerful thing.

I push a little deeper, giving her body time to adjust, to tighten and clench around my cock.

"Christ you're tight." I drop my forehead to hers. "It feels so fucking good."

She makes a noise deep in her throat. A noise I'm beginning to associate with her deepest pleasure. "Tell me?" she whispers. "Tell me how it feels?"

Jesus, she wants me to talk dirty. I'm thirty seconds from completely humiliating myself and…I close my eyes and start to whisper.

"You're tight." I press my lips to her throat. "Wet." I scrape my teeth over her ear, nipping, biting. "Hot."

She spreads her thighs a little more, and it takes everything I have not to push inside her. She rocks her hips, urging me deeper, pressing her thighs against my hips, urging me fully *home*.

I slide deeper inside her, slow, smooth, hoping, praying that for once, it doesn't hurt. I'm lost in a sense of completion, of being one with a partner in the deepest of connections.

She brushes her lips against my neck. "Please," she whispers.

And then I start to move, drowning in the sparks and fire from her tight body that grips me as I spiral out in a million starbursts of raw, intense pleasure.

CHAPTER 23

Parker

HE IS WRAPPED AROUND ME, one thigh pressed between mine, his hips flush against me. His scent surrounds me, penetrating my skin like the heat from his body. I never want to move again. I want to stay here forever and pretend that the world outside doesn't exist.

That I'm just a girl, asking a boy to love her.

But I can't.

And Eli deserves to know why.

Because everyone should bare their dark and twisted trauma right after the glow from amazing, mind-blowing sex starts to fade.

"My mom died when I was sixteen." He shifts behind me, his arm tightening around my belly. It's a subtle movement but I know he's listening. "My dad told me he found her in their bed. Said she died in her sleep." I swallow and close my eyes. "I didn't believe him but her death...it destroyed him." His fingers are strong and steady on my forearm. "She overdosed. In hindsight, it makes sense. She'd have these episodes where she'd slur her speech or stagger around the house." The dark tunnel of the memories leads me only toward further darkness. But Eli deserves to know. Maybe then, he can understand why I'm trapped in my life.

"Jesus, Parker."

I drive on, needing to get everything out. Needing to excise the wound just once more before I cover it up and pretend there's no scar. "She'd filed for divorce a few weeks before she died." My voice is steady, surprising me. Like this isn't my story but some sad tale about someone else's life. "She made the national news. For a whole week. There was sympathy, at least at first. The press followed me to school, asking me if I knew my mom was an addict."

"You were a child."

"Rich people's kids never get to be children. It's a very First World problem."

He nuzzles my neck. "Don't trivialize how hard that is. Just because you're not starving and homeless doesn't mean your problems aren't real."

I'm not sure how to respond to that. "My dad didn't think so. I started acting out. My friend Meaghan and I started partying, hard. I wanted to hurt him. To embarrass him." I take a deep breath. "It was a universally stupid thing to try with someone like my father."

"What did he do to you?"

"I left. I tried to anyway. I convinced Meaghan to leave with me."

"Where were you going to go?"

"I don't know. I think I was hoping my aunt would take us in. She refused. And then my father found us."

His body is tense behind me now, his breathing rough. "He hurt you."

"I'd just lost my mom. And then I lost my dad, too. He stopped talking to me. Pretended I wasn't there. Married his new wife within a year." The words aren't easy, don't take away the pain. The words I need aren't breaking past the blockade in my chest. "I tried everything I knew to get him to see me. To remember he had a daughter." A final deep, shuddering breath. The tightness in my chest breaks up a little. "When I met Davis, it was like I suddenly had my dad back. After ten years, he was finally able to be in the same room as me. Finally, able to talk to me. It was like being born again, having him back." I swallow hard. "But it's always about Davis. I'm a means to a son for him." I thread my fingers with his, needing to remind myself that this is real, that I'm lying here with Eli and that for a brief moment, everything is all right in my world. Even as I rip the scars off old wounds, I'm with him.

"Then I got this sad little dick pic from a sixty-year-old man. One of my father's closest friends, of all people, who was supposed to give me an internship to help me compete for the executive management program." I laugh at the thought of that terrible image, burned for all eternity into my memory whether I want it or not. "Something inside me snapped. I wanted out. And Davis blamed me."

"Wait, he blamed you for your future boss sending you a dick pic?"

"Pretty much. He just saw the picture from the unknown number that popped up in my notifications."

"Charming people you hang around with," he says dryly.

I've almost forgotten how good his voice sounds in my ear. How warm and rich and *real*. Everything about Eli is authentic. I twist in his arms, turning until my breasts tease the crisp hair on his chest. Until I can look him in the eye. "It's what I love about you. You mean what you say. You believe in what you do. You didn't turn me away." I cradle his face, kissing him lightly. "But now you know why I'm stuck. Davis won't let me leave. It's too embarrassing for him to get dumped. And even if I tried, the media would catch wind and resurrect the ghost of my mother."

He tugs me even closer, tucking my head beneath his chin. His heartbeat is steady and strong beneath my cheek, reminding me that this isn't just a dream. This is real, even if it's only a brief moment that will become a memory. It's a memory I'll hold on to. This time with him. This connection.

"What do you want?" He presses his lips to the top of my head. "If you could have anything in the world, what would you want?"

I close my eyes and breathe him in. In theory, it's such a simple question. To imagine the best possible future and ignore the most likely one. To hold on to an ideal, a fantasy as an escape from the reality that's dark and full of emptiness. "To stay."

Eli

IT'S UNREASONABLE. Her reasons are completely irrational and based on emotion. But those are the most effective prisons.

None of that matters, because for her, the bars are as real as anything in our world. She lives in her own iron cage, created bar by bar by two insecure men obsessed with control and power and how they look in the press.

Her father's also not just a handsome face with a winning smile. The cage he's built around his daughter reveals a ruthlessness about him that shouldn't be ignored.

In any campaign, you need to understand the enemy. And I have a perfect opportunity to observe him at his party.

I know how to walk in his world, how to blend in. Even with my beard and tattoos, I can still play the game.

It's a game I've avoided for years. The risk attached to my past is well-hidden, but it would only take one industrious reporter to connect the dots and that's just operating on the assumption that people don't ask Google the right question.

For Parker, though, I'll step back into the world I've walked away from.

I'll talk to her father tonight, see what I can learn about her soon-to-be ex-fiancé. Ply him with expensive whiskey. Men will always talk over whiskey, especially men like her father. They need to brag, need the world to see how shiny and bright they are to hide the pitiful man they see in the mirror.

"You can, you know." I wait until her face is lifted toward mine and I drink from her, sipping at her lips in a gentle, coaxing kiss. "Stay."

I need her to feel the word, not just hear it.

"Does it bother you? Lying here with a woman engaged to another man?" Her words break now and it shatters my heart hearing the pain in her voice.

"No." I press my lips to her shoulder, avoiding the urge to nip at her. "Because your heart doesn't belong to him." I trace my tongue over her, blowing on the moist skin. "Pretend you can do whatever you want. What would that look like?"

Her breath is a sigh against my mouth. My fingers trace the length of her spine. Her body is stiff and unyielding.

"I never really thought about it."

I'm taking a dangerous risk right now, deliberately mixing arousal with fear and uncertainty. "Try." I shift again, pressing closer without really moving. The sensation of her skin against mine, the softness of her body, is pure sensual overload. I could stay here forever, just touching her.

"I'd be cut off. Financially."

"You do have expensive tastes," I nibble on her ear. "I don't know how much those leggings you like to wear cost but they're sexy as hell."

She makes a noise in her throat. My distraction is working. I can feel her purring. "I'd have to find a job. Which will be impossible once my father tells his friends not to hire me."

"Why do you need to work in a company tied to your father?" She subtly rocks her hips against my leg. It's torture not slipping my hand between her thighs. I want to feel her wetness coat my fingers, feel her swell beneath my touch.

"What else am I qualified for?"

"I can think of at least six things. Three of them involve marketing and whiskey."

She smiles up at me. "Just because I know the brands doesn't mean I know how to sell them."

"You catch on pretty quickly."

"Not quickly enough to pay the lease on my apartment when it comes due in six months."

I trace a small circle on the swell of her breast. Her nipple tightens, shrinking into a dusty pink tip. I trace my index finger around it and am rewarded with another rock of her hips against me. This time, she brushes against my erection, leaving a light kiss of moisture against my cock.

She surprises me then, slipping her hand between our bodies to stroke me. Her fist is tight around me, just enough pressure to draw out the pleasure of her touch.

"That gives you six months to figure something out." It's harder to think now with her hand fisted around my cock. She rubs her thumb over the tip, spreading the wetness across the crown. "Jesus that feels good," I whisper.

"Does it?"

"Fuck yeah." She's shifted the rules of the game on me. In an instant, I've gone from teasing her and touching her to being teased, being touched. She urges me onto my back and slips on top.

She's fucking perfection. Her breasts are heavy and full, swaying gently as she moves her thighs apart to straddle my hips.

She's glistening between her thighs, already wet. I want to put my mouth on her, to feel her from the inside as she comes.

She lowers her hips, touching her damp curls to the ridge of my cock. A feather-light tease. One I cannot look away from. She sinks lower, her lips spreading to surround me, slipping down my length, coating me in her wet heat. "Jesus, do that again."

She obliges me, sliding her sex over mine again, a delicious, sensual friction. The sight of my dick slipping through her slick folds is an erotic torment, blinding me with intense pleasure. She slides again, teasing my cock at her tight opening.

Her eyes are closed, her hips moving more quickly, her heat driving me closer to the edge.

She reaches between our bodies, lifting me until I'm there, just there. Her body sucks at me, drawing me deeper as she sinks smoothly onto my cock, inch by glorious, tight inch.

Her palms brace against my chest as she stills for a moment.

"Does it hurt?"

She leans down, lifting her hips, sliding off my cock, then lowering back once more. "It feels amazing."

And then she starts to move.

CHAPTER 24

Eli

DEACON AND KELSEY both agreed to be enlisted into the evening's festivities, and Kelsey's wearing a long-sleeved, white button-down blouse to hide the thorns and roses that twist over her arms.

The three of us whipped together a drink menu and packed out the van I use for catering yet again.

I love them both for their willingness to bust their asses for me at a moment's notice. But that's what's great about my place. It's really ours. I swear to all the powers that be that I will do right by them.

Always.

We're at an old mansion on the western edge of Durham. It sits on several acres and when I looked it up, I discovered it was one of the few original houses that survived the destruction of the Civil War. It's been restored to its original splendor, and near its entrance, I'm surprised to find a monument to the slaves that died building the original house and who worked the land.

"Well, that's interesting," Kelsey murmurs dryly as we're unloading the whiskey.

Deacon lifts one eyebrow. "Because an *I'm sorry* monument makes everything better?"

"But of course." Kelsey pats his shoulder gently. "Now is not the time to critique our beneficiaries' intentions. Down that path lies nonpayment for services rendered."

I smile. Kelsey is so fucking pragmatic sometimes it's scary.

We get the bar set up, putting the higher-end whiskey literally higher up. It creates the perception of something out of reach and feeds the need to be seen ordering it.

People, wealthy or poor, are remarkably simple creatures sometimes.

Parker will be here later. I'd kissed her and followed her down to the bar where I talked her through my accounts receivable and how I've been focusing on building my brand. Simple yet elegant, The Pint is a name that's both familiar and obvious, but the logo is written in old English letters, drawing a connection between old world and new.

And then I'd urged her to go home and get ready for tonight. She needs to shine and most importantly, she needs to be one hundred percent on. There's no room for error in perception.

She isn't convinced she can leave, that she can walk away from the only world she knows. But the seed has been planted. She is thinking about it now, dreaming of the impossible.

Tonight is for me to learn more about the players in the game. To figure out how to exploit any openings.

I've opted tonight for a white button-down, rolled at the sleeves. I know my audience, and the slight rule-breaking of exposing my inked arms will draw more eyes and whispers. Once the whispers start, I'll be holding court steadily for the rest of the evening with the wives who want to know the man behind the beard. The tattoos are an opening for conversation, drawing their wealthy eyes to my marked skin.

I can smile and wave with the best of them. That's also why I've got Deacon and Kelsey. I want the smiling and the drinking.

There are two opportunities for The Pint tonight.

The first is purely selfish—we do this right and it's more business. I've got business cards on the bar, easy enough to pick up. Providing alcohol service to expensive parties wasn't on the business plan for another five years, but I'd be a fool to ignore the opportunity that's presenting itself. I have no moral principles against taking advantage of meeting Bennington Hauser's contacts tonight, and any doors that serving them might open.

The second is to get to know Hauser better. To figure out what Parker needs to do to slip free of him and the life he wants her to lead.

Both should be relatively easy to handle.

Until Parker walks in wearing a cream cocktail dress that is fucking stunning.

She's brilliant and smiling, polished and poised. I watch her for a moment as she shakes hands, laughing at offhand remarks. If I hadn't spent the afternoon with her, I'd never guess she was anything other than completely at ease.

My balls tighten watching her. I can see the curves beneath that dress. I know how she feels in my hands, her hips spread over mine as she rides me.

"Careful, loverboy, you're going to embarrass yourself." Deacon's voice is a gentle reminder that eye-fucking the guests is never a good policy.

I make a rough noise and look away. "Thanks."

"It hurts, doesn't it?" He's adjusting the mid-priced whiskey, turning the labels in a way that highlights their contrasting colors.

"What's that?"

"Falling this hard. Catches you by surprise."

I look down, adjusting the card reader in an effort to keep my fingers busy. "It's complicated."

"It always is." He leans on the counter. "The question is, what are you going to do with a woman like that? She's not going to want to be chained to a bar, working fifteen, twenty hours a day."

I steal another peek at Parker. She's turned to one side, a polite smile on her lips, her fingers wrapped effortlessly around a champagne flute filled with a pomegranate champagne that Deacon concocted for tonight's event.

"She can stay or go or do whatever she wants." I focus on setting up.

"Spoken like a man who doesn't sound like he's used to letting go."

Deacon isn't wrong often. He's not wrong now, but I can't tell him that. Because as much as it hurts to admit, I'll eventually have to let her go.

She won't stay. She can't. I might know how to move in her world, but she doesn't belong in mine.

I just can't leave her trapped.

Her father walks in and it's like watching all the oxygen get sucked into a vacuum. Everyone gravitates toward him.

Even Parker, who smiles and kisses his cheek without ever revealing to the world the truth of her life.

Parker

MY FATHER SMILES WARMLY. You'd have to know what you're looking for to see how irritated he is with me.

It's not his eyes that give it away. No, it would be too easy to spot his mood if the tell was in his eyes.

It's in his jaw. The tension in his smile radiates down his jaw.

"I'm glad you could find it in your schedule to make it," he says, kissing me lightly on the cheek.

"I'm sorry I worried you. I was deeply engaged on a project." I wonder how Eli would feel about being called a project. I sip the pomegranate champagne to hide my smile from my father.

"Have you seen Davis? He told me you spoke at the fundraiser."

It's hard to hate my father. He says all the right things and asks all the right questions. But none of it is genuine. It's all meant to make him look like something he isn't: a decent human being.

"We spoke." I don't want to talk about my future sentence. Not when I can still feel Eli surrounding me.

"And? Are you coming to the city next weekend for Lainey's birthday party?"

"I don't think I can." I scan the room, looking for any sign of Davis. "Dad, can I talk to you about something?"

"Sure."

He's wary now but if I don't do this here, I'll never get his attention. "I'm not sure if Davis is being honest with you about…everything."

My father waves at the hostess, smiling brilliantly in the way that men who are familiar with how money moves the world often do. This is a party for the men he needs to make sure his bids on government contracts win. He's not a politician but he damn sure knows how to work a room like he was one.

"What do you mean?"

"Well, remember a few weeks ago when your company got in hot water with CNN for that Facebook post about veterans and guns? About how it was insensitive and exploitative?"

He's listening, even if he's busy taking stock of who is in the room. Especially those donors attached to big dollar signs. "I certainly don't need the reminder. Where are you going with this?"

"Davis…didn't delete his own post when he shared it. He left it up."

Finally, my father turns to look fully at me. It's unnerving seeing the calculations behind his eyes. "So?"

"So the media were able to get the picture because he didn't delete his post. I can't help but wonder why he didn't take it down as soon as you directed your communications chief to take it down." I lean in and kiss him on the cheek. "I'm sure it's nothing. It just felt a little off. I said something to him and he finally took the post down. But it just felt…weird having to tell him."

The entire snafu with the errant Facebook post was something trivial. Incredibly minor, in the grand scheme of things. But it's a brilliant way to get my father to start questioning whether my match with Davis is the right alliance.

It doesn't get me out of the situation immediately. But I've planted a seed, if nothing else.

"I'll talk to him." He waves at someone behind me. "You should come home next weekend."

"I have work. My internship duties call." I take another sip from the gloriously sweet drink that has just enough alcohol to loosen me up.

My father tips his chin at me, his eyes glittering darkly. "You never did tell me why you turned down Montgomery's offer. It would look much better on your application for the executive program than some bar in Durham, no matter how good the whiskey is."

I wonder how hard it is for him to not choke on the disdain. It practically drips from his words.

"I wanted to do something different." He'd never believe me that his long-time friend sent me a sad picture of his dick. He'd ask me what I'd done to lead him on. Or why I was trying to ruin the reputation of a man like Montgomery Carlisle.

There's no reason to even waste my breath. No, there are other ways to deal with my father and his so-called friends.

"Which reminds me. You've got a bunch of events planned in the coming months in the local area. I was thinking a great way to shore up local favor is to use local vendors whenever possible—smaller ones. Spread the wealth around, so to speak." I tip my glass toward the bar where Eli is pouring a tiny drop of water in a glass of whiskey. "You've seen what The Pint can do on last-minute notice. He has one of the most exquisite whiskey collections I've ever seen. If you add him to the event programs, you'll curry local favor and have access to some rare whiskey and unique blends."

"What are you proposing?"

No wasting time or words. "Put him on contract. Have him agree to support every event in a two-hundred-mile radius. You get guaranteed service at a bargain."

"How do you figure paying every month for a service I don't use is a good investment?"

"How much is tonight running you?"

"I've set the tab for twenty-five thousand."

I run the numbers quickly in my head. "You've got five events in the next six months. You offer fifteen thousand a month, plus fifteen percent overhead expenses for every thousand dollars you go over. You save in the long run and Eli's whiskey ends up in more people's glasses. It's brand expansion for him and a bargain for you."

"Won't he lose money?"

"I have my doubts that Eli ever loses at anything."

My father looks sharply at me. "You've been thinking about this for a while."

"I paid attention in my marketing classes. There isn't a comparable whiskey collection anywhere in the South. You need to present yourself as one of the people. Whiskey is a good way to do that, while still allowing you to signal to your donors that you're a winner."

He takes a sip from his own glass. "Talk to Eugene and run the numbers. Your back-of-the-napkin calculations sound a little sketchy."

I smile up at him and for once, it is one hundred percent genuine. "I'll do that."

One of my father's politician friends walks up, demanding an audience. I back away smoothly, melting into obscurity as quickly as I can.

"What are you smiling about?"

My internal victory dance comes to a record-screeching halt at Davis's voice in my ear. "Just had an enjoyable chat with my father." My smile is tight now and it requires genuine effort to keep it looking natural instead of forced.

I may chip a tooth before the night is over at this rate.

"You look lovely tonight. Did you do something different with your hair?"

I had Eli's fingers threaded in it. Somehow I don't think Davis would appreciate that response. "New shampoo."

"Have you checked your email today?"

I sip my drink and suddenly wish it were a hell of a lot stronger. "Anything interesting?"

He's going to tell me. He's just going to drag it out a bit before he does. It's his way of lording what he knows over me for as long as possible.

"You should really do more research about the people you choose to associate with." He hands me his phone.

It's a photo of me with Eli the other night. Sitting a little too close. Looking a little too comfortable. The innuendo in the image is bad enough. The headline makes my stomach pitch. Congressman's Fiancée involved with War Criminal.

The words are a lead weight around my neck. I feel ill as I skim the text.

"Ready to come home yet? Or do you want to continue hanging out with your own personal Lieutenant Calley?"

I forward myself the article, hand him back his phone, and drink the rest of my champagne. "Does my father know?" I'm going to need something a hell of a lot stronger to get through the rest of the evening.

"It hasn't run yet. I've asked the reporter to hold off until we have time to prepare a statement."

I open the document on my phone. "What do you think is an appropriate response?"

"Complete disavowal. You didn't know there were this many skeletons in his closet. You need to start distancing yourself from him, starting tonight."

Someone once told me that nobody is a hero all the time. There are only moments, and what you do in those moments matters more than a lifetime of other actions.

I look up at Davis. At the future I see looking back at me from the edge of the abyss.

And I stand there, too afraid to take the leap.

CHAPTER 25

Eli

"My daughter tells me you've got quite the taste in whiskey."

I try not to choke after hearing those words. I'm quite positive Bennington Hauser would not want to know even the slightest thing about what his daughter and I were up to with regards to whiskey.

I'm not even amused at the idea of leading this conversation into double-entendre territory. I can't risk it. I have to play ball if I'm going to figure out a way to help Parker.

"I learned a long time ago that if you're going to do something, do it to the best of your ability."

"And that includes building your brand on other people's whiskey?"

"I'm good at finding the hidden jewels out there. Less so at brewing my own." I raise my glass to him. "I find it's generally good practice to play to my strengths and keep others around to compensate for my weaknesses."

Bennington nods sagely. "Smart." He studies me for a moment, and somehow I'm convinced he's also scanning the room around us, even though his eyes never waver from my face. "My daughter had an interesting proposition for me tonight. I wanted to hear it from you, though."

"What proposition is that?" Dear lord, this conversation is going to be the death of me. All I can think of if I close my eyes is Parker's hips spread across mine, my cock disappearing into her tight, sweet body.

Jesus, can I not think about that in front of her father? He might be a selfish bastard but damn it, it's just all kinds of wrong to be thinking about the man's daughter that way while he's standing two feet in front of me.

And I really don't want to have to duck into a bathroom and adjust my pants. I'm not fucking twelve anymore.

"She proposes I offer you a retainer. Guaranteed contract for services provided, paid out in monthly increments."

I frown, wondering what the hell Parker is thinking. I can't afford to go on a contract for a set amount. I'd lose my ass the first time the bar tab went over the contracted amount. "I'm not sure that's feasible. I appreciate her thinking of me but—"

Hauser holds up his hand. "The events would be much smaller than this. Much more intimate. Contract would be very generous terms and provide guaranteed income for you for limited engagements."

"What's the catch?"

"No catch. It will all be spelled out in the contract terms."

I can't help but feel like I'm making a deal with the devil. "I'll have my attorney take a look at it."

We shake on it. I wish I could say that I feel like I've just sold my soul, but he's a smooth operator. Knows how to put someone at ease and that's an impressive skill set to be able to pull one over on me, especially when I'm looking for it. "Parker has a hell of a good head for business."

"That's about all she's good at since her mother died."

His comment sounds off the cuff and catches me off guard. It's the kind of comment you make to family friends, not future business associates. "I'm sorry to hear that."

He shrugs and takes a sip of his whiskey. "I've been a little too indulgent with her. Letting her come down here instead of going to Yale. Letting her pick her internship instead of insisting she work for Carlisle Industries. Montgomery Carlisle's name on her résumé would have opened any door in the Beltway for her but instead, she's down here, learning about whiskey."

"Well, sir, I for one am grateful for the opportunity to work with her. She's asked some great questions that have prompted me to reevaluate how I'm doing things and the analytics she's developed combined with her ideas for a marketing plan is game changing. She's an incredible asset."

He scans the room before he looks back at me. All of a sudden I'm reminded of standing for inspection in front of the First Captain my plebe year. Like all my sins were exposed for all the world to see. "She's a real prize. I get compliments all the time on her accomplishments. She's fantastic to have at events like these because everyone wants to talk to her. She's really terrific."

There's something there, beneath his words. I can't put my finger on it, but I tuck the conversation away to replay it later. He's most likely just a father bragging about his daughter. But something doesn't feel right about this entire exchange.

"And here's the man of the hour. Eli Winter, I'd like you to meet Davis Harcourt, Parker's fiancé."

It takes every ounce of restraint not to knock his teeth out of his head. And the moment he opens his mouth, I realize it's going to take a lot more patience than I may have. Davis isn't nearly as smooth as his future father-in-law. In fact, he's exactly the kind of smarmy and condescending douchebag that I hated in my previous life.

"Winter. Didn't I see an article that said you were in the Army?"

The way Davis says it sends the hair on the back of my neck standing straight up. "I was."

"You'd think a man with your background would be less... prone to seeking media attention."

I shrug and do my damnedest to keep my expression blank. I don't know what he knows, but he knows a hell of a lot more than nothing. And that makes him dangerous. To me. To my business. To the people who are counting on me to make this business work. "I'm used to dealing with the media. I had a lot of practice in Iraq."

Davis smirks and doesn't even try to hide the asshole. "I bet you did. You should be careful. Skeletons have a way of finding their way out of the closet."

"You really ought to follow your own advice," I say mildly. Fuck this guy in his three-thousand-dollar suit and peroxide smile. The damage is already done from my skeletons. Nothing I do can change the outcome from any of them. But Davis has a lot more than me to lose. "No one cares about a bar owner in a college town, but a junior congressman should probably be more careful with who he hurts in his life." I smile coldly. "The arm you grab today may be connected to the ass you have to kiss tomorrow."

His smile doesn't falter but his eyes give away the quiet slice of my direct hit. "Indeed."

And then I'm alone as they both step away, wondering just what he meant and why I suddenly feel like all of this is running too close to the edge.

That everything I've worked for over the last five years is about to go up in blood-soaked flames, resurrected from the desert of Iraq.

Parker

I'M NOT DRUNK, but I wish I were. My stomach twists every time I look at the draft article on my phone. I slip out of the party, needing space to figure out what the hell all of this means and what I'm supposed to do now.

"You look like you're having a real shit evening, as shit evenings go."

Meaghan strides over on her four-inch heels and sinks onto the bench next to me. The garden is a peaceful spot for this unwanted reunion. Surrounded by hydrangeas and rose bushes and a thousand species I can't recognize, it's still nice to see my once-upon-a-time partner in crime.

"It's up there on the list of top ten bad evenings." I glance over at her. "I didn't know you were going to be here."

She shrugs and sips her drink. I wonder how many she's had. Or how early she started drinking.

She'd always been a bit wild, but after we got caught running away things got really bad with her. I thought things weren't great for me, but Meaghan...yeah, she had it a hell of a lot worse. Her mother is a special kind of evil, and unfortunately Meaghan has started taking on some of her mother's more unsavory personality traits.

Which is just one of the reasons why we aren't really close anymore. Not like we had been, once upon a time.

"I'm not going home this summer," Meaghan says.

"Say what? How? When?"

This is news. And when I say news, I mean earth-shattering, major life-altering event-worthy news. "I want out. Away from my mom and her psycho boy toy. Away from all of it."

"How, though? She's not going to just let you go."

Meaghan smiles and for once, she looks like my friend used to, before the drinking and the drugs started taking her away from me. "I'm getting her to put me in rehab here. Outpatient program for a year. She's going to fund every last dime and in the meantime, I'm going to figure out how to do this adulting thing." She looks at me apologetically. "Which means I'm going to need your help because I want to actually start taking classes instead of paying someone to take them for me, and start being a grownup, and I really have no clue where to even start."

I shift on the cold stone bench. "Are you serious? You're going to leave home? And your mom is going to just…let you go? But…"

The night we tried to leave, we were sixteen. We had a pocket full of cash, our cell phones, and no fucking idea where we were going or what we were going to do. We'd crashed at our friend Bodhi's pad in Alexandria and thought we'd made the break.

That was the night I found out just how bad Meaghan's drug problem was. And how determined our parents were to keep us under control. There were going to be no *Girls Gone Wild* videos getting made with us as the stars.

"I know I screwed up," she says quietly. "Bad. And I lost you as a result." She looks down at her perfectly manicured hands. "I've missed you. I don't know what this thing is we've been doing the last five years but it's not friendship. I want our friendship back. The real one. Before everything got screwed up."

I sit for a moment, frozen in time and space as her words sink into my rational brain and into the part of me that misses my friend dearly.

"Please say something because otherwise, this is going to get even more awkward than it already is."

I smile and thread my arm in hers, resting my head on her shoulder like I used to once upon a time, after my mom died and my world ended. "I've missed you," I whisper.

"Me too." Her cheek presses against my head. "So what's this I hear about you working at a bar? Why didn't you go work for Montgomery Carlisle?"

I sigh and hand her my cell phone and show her Mr. Carlisle and Mr. Carlisle Junior in all their glory. "Ew! What is that?"

"That's the reason why I'm not working for him."

"Is that his…junk?"

I breathe out deliberately. "Yep."

Her reaction is not what I expect. She covers her mouth with her hand and laughs. And then I'm laughing at the absurdity of it because in hindsight, it's really just sad.

"Working at The Pint is the best thing that's ever happened to me. It's…amazing. It's fun and they actually care about each other there."

"So it's like *Cheers*?"

I smile because I'd forgotten that we used to skip school and watch *Cheers* marathons our freshman year. "I think it's better than *Cheers*. You'll have to come in and check it out."

"I might need to talk to the owner about a job."

I smirk, thinking of her fending off Mr. Blowjob reporter from the other night. "It's definitely got some unique challenges."

"So if things are going so well, how come you look so upset?"

My phone's screen is blank now. I don't want to show her the hit piece that Davis sent me. I haven't figured out how to tackle this problem.

"It's complicated," I tell her. Because while I love the idea of having my friend back, I'm also a cynic. I want to trust her. I want her back. But we have our history and trust takes time to rebuild.

But this? This is about Eli. Eli who dared me to take a leap, to not stay trapped in my life.

I can't process what I've read.

I don't even know how to ask Eli about it.

What do I do if the story is true? What do I say?

I stare at my phone, trapped, once again, between terrible choices.

CHAPTER 26

Eli

I DON'T SEE Parker again for the rest of the evening. I'm too busy to do more than occasionally scan the room quickly for her.

"Dude, we've got a fucking problem." Kelsey grabs my arm and I follow her into an empty hallway. "Your girl's boy toy? I heard him talking to our girl."

I'm already braced for the worst, but the look on Kelsey's face suggests it's worse than I expect. "So?"

"Any reason why your name should be mentioned in the same sentence as war crimes?"

I swallow hard. "Possibly."

She sets her jaw, and in that instant I can see Sergeant Ryder standing in front of me, no nonsense and all business and fiercely protective of those who she sees as hers. "Well, we're fucked, then, because the words war criminal and article and your name were all mentioned in the same sentence. Want to tell me what it was about? Before it blows up all over CNN?"

"There's nothing to talk about. No one cares about war crimes in a war that few people even remember we're even fighting."

"They do when a defense contractor's daughter is working for a man who could be held responsible for them." She braces her hands on her hips, and I can see her calculating. I need her to stand down.

"This is my problem. I'll figure it out. Go get these folks to spend more money on expensive whiskey." I grip her shoulder, needing to get away and start developing courses of action. "Trust me?"

She's clearly not happy but keeps her displeasure to herself, offering instead a mock salute. "Roger that, sir."

The trust in her eyes as she turns back to the party is sobering. She doesn't question whether I've done something wrong. Doesn't care even if I did.

It's humbling, the loyalty she just demonstrated.

I head back to the bar, glad-handing the wives of sponsors and chatting up future customers but there's a stone in my belly now, a tight knot of dread weighing me down.

I've always thought I was prepared for this day. I knew it would come. I've spent years building ties to the community, to my suppliers and distributors, hoping that when it came, they would look past the allegations and remember that I'm still the same person.

But civilians are funny about things that happen at war. You never know how someone will react to the idea that bad shit happens in war and no, sometimes, commanders don't know everything that's going on in their unit.

I honestly can't say how any of my suppliers are going to react if this breaks big. I always imagined it would break as a long read that no one actually read. That I could face the jury of public opinion when people were otherwise occupied thinking about the latest celebrity gossip.

I pour a shot of Laphroiag and add a single drop of water. The smoky taste pulls me out of the dread, but now my go-to whiskey stirs other memories. Memories of Parker's thighs spread before me, her body warm beneath my tongue, mixing with the whiskey.

The whiskey is mild, sliding down my throat, easing the knot just a little.

There's nothing I can do to change the past. And this isn't just about me anymore.

I suppose my history is surfacing because I'm somehow tied to Parker.

I could lose everything if this blows up big enough.

Not just the bar.

But what the bar means to me, to Kelsey, Deacon. Noah. Josh. All of my merry band of misfit toys.

And Parker. I've only just stepped out of the darkness into the light with her, only just started to believe that maybe there's more to this life than taking care of soldiers.

The thought of losing her...the knot in my chest is back and no amount of Laphroaig can break it free.

I see her across the crowded room.

And she knows. I can see it in her eyes, in the disappointment and uncertainty looking back at me.

Because I can do nothing less, I follow her from the room. To the garden that leads away from the guests and the party and the silken splendor of the world she has been trying to so desperately escape.

She doesn't stop.

"So that's it? You're just going to walk away?" I can't keep the anger from my voice. At least it masks the hurt.

She stops but doesn't turn around. "How would you like to explain this to me? In any way that makes sense?"

"You're not giving me much of a chance to explain anything by walking away."

Her voice is quiet. "How? How can you explain away something like war crimes?"

Parker

I'VE NEVER SEEN a man like Eli go white as a sheet but he is deathly pale. His mouth forms a grim line beneath his beard.

I can barely stand there.

"I did not commit any war cimes." His eyes flash dangerously. There is darkness in those words. Danger and defense. "I was in command of men that did."

"What's the difference?"

"The difference is between ordering a war crime and stopping one." He drags his hands through his hair. "But you wouldn't know that. You're so hell-bent on seeing what you want to see, you condemn first, ask questions later."

"That's not fair. I don't understand your world. The Army. The life you led before you came here."

He turns away, arms folded over his chest. "You know me. Is it too much to ask that you trust me enough to ask a question first? To get some goddamned clarification first?"

"Clarification over what? Prisoners were shot. Your men shot them."

Eli

IT'S SO easy to judge, isn't it?" I'm daring her to look at me, to see me, not whatever bastardized version she's read about. "You don't know what it's like to make life-and-death decisions. To know that by ordering that investigation, I cost some of my men their lives because I took combat-tested soldiers off the streets."

"So that excuses this?"

"I stopped it! I fucking stopped it as soon as I found out. I didn't even hesitate to report it higher." I'm standing in front of her now, daring her to look beyond the words on her screen and see me. But she doesn't. Maybe she can't. Right then, I don't care. "You're just running away again. It's easier to walk away and never look back than to unpack some uncomfortable truths about the people in your life."

"Maybe I am. But maybe this is something worth running away from."

"And maybe, what we've got is something worth standing and fighting for."

She smiles at me and it's filled with a lifetime's worth of sadness and disappointment. "Maybe we did. But that trust thing you talk so much about?" She pauses, rubbing her hands over her upper arms. "You don't get to demand it without giving it."

"Parker..." I need her to stay. To ask me questions. To let me tell her the truth that's buried in the story that's going to be out there.

But she slips around me and keeps walking.

Disappearing into the garden and away from me and the life I tried to build on a lie.

CHAPTER 27

Parker

I'M NOT REALLY sure how it got to this. How losing Eli hurts as bad as it does, like a part of my soul has been ripped out and there's just an aching hole left. It's the emptiness that destroys me the most. The realization that there's nothing that will fill the gap.

It's even more depressing realizing that I have nowhere to go. I can't go to The Pint. I can't talk to Eli right now.

I can't call my father. He'd tell me to be glad that Davis found out about Eli's past before things got too complicated.

But they're already complicated. They were that first night I walked into The Pint and all but asked him to fuck me and he said no. It was supposed to be an uncomplicated hookup. I can't believe how hard I fell for him. Because he showed me a little bit of kindness and gave me a place to belong, really belong.

I walked away without giving him a chance to explain any of it.

I just can't wrap my brain around how he could justify what I read. How can he explain it away? Because if he can't, then he's responsible for those terrible things.

The article said "war crimes". "Court-martial". I don't know much about the military, but I'm pretty sure those two things are not fucking good. How can there possibly be a rational explanation for any of it?

I squeeze my eyes shut, wishing I hadn't spent an entire semester arguing about violence. Now that violence is all too real, tied to a man that I gave my heart to. Irony is one cold bitch, I tell you.

Crying hurts too damn much. And I've spilled more than enough tears over the screwed-up men in my life.

And what does that say about me?

It says I'm tired of this shit.

I breathe out hard. And pick up my phone.

Davis answers before it even rings once. "Well hello," he says mildly.

I don't want to listen to his voice, don't want to pretend that everything is normal. It's not. And if I'm honest with myself, it hasn't been for a long time. "What I can't figure out is why you'd let this article run. It makes you look like an idiot."

He makes a noise on the other end. "I don't need to have this published in order to get what I want out of the deal."

"And that is?"

"You. You're smart. You're pretty. And you're the daughter of one of the biggest power brokers in the capital. You're going to stop these childish games and come home."

The distaste in my mouth sours to something vile. "And if I don't play along?"

"I make a few calls. And your lover boy gets blasted for being the trigger-happy war criminal that he is. He loses all of his suppliers. His business shuts down. And you have to come home anyway. Either way, you come home. The question becomes how much damage do you want to leave behind you when you leave?"

I press my forehead into my palm, sadness and fatigue clouding my head and making it hard to think. There has to be a way through this. There has to be.

I just can't think of it at the moment.

Davis breaks the silence. "I'll call you tomorrow. I expect your decision then."

It's amazing how much his voice reminds me of Emperor Palpatine. Only without the cool red lightning fingers.

I drag my comforter over my head, needing twelve hours of sleep before my brain starts to function again.

But sleep is apparently not on the agenda because someone is beating on my door like the building is on fire.

What will I do if it's Eli on the other side?

Whoever it is, though, isn't going away. The banging intensifies to the point that I'm sure the door is coming off its hinges if I don't open it. I sit up, brushing my hair out of my face, and debate whether or not I should do anything more than tie it back before answering the door.

If it's Eli…if it's Eli, judging from the way he's pounding on the door, the conversation isn't going to end any way that would call for brushed teeth and sexy panties.

I shrug on a sweatshirt and pad to the door, yanking it open. Part of me hopes it's Eli, even if I have no clue what I'll do if it is.

I reluctantly open the door, to find that it's definitely not someone I'd need to brush my teeth and put on sexy undies for.

Kelsey is standing on my welcome mat, her hair tied up in a twisted bun, her expression shifting between concern and irritation. "You look like shit," she says, thrusting a beer into my hand.

The force of her greeting, such as it is, takes me back a step. "And here I was just contemplating my underwear choices before answering the door."

She pauses, frowns, then smiles. I hope that's a smile, anyway. Otherwise I'm about to be missing some teeth. I have a funny feeling she hits harder than Davis ever would.

But she doesn't hit me, doesn't lash out. Instead, she stands there, a bundle of pent-up energy, practically vibrating with a need to move. "Okay seriously, you need to let me in because you have to help us unfuck this, and I'm out of my league with you people."

Well now I'm curious. "Unfuck what?"

"Whatever happened between you and Eli that's had him barricaded in his office since last night."

I take a step back and let her into my apartment.

Which, thankfully, isn't completely destroyed. Except for the milk that I left on the counter at some point. Or the empty container from Chipotle that thankfully hasn't started growing legs and trying to take over the world.

Or the empty wine bottles.

Okay, maybe it's as bad as it looks.

"What happened?" I ask, forgetting my manners because I'm standing there in a ratty sweatshirt and unbrushed hair. I'm in no shape to serve tea and crumpets. And what the hell is a crumpet, anyway?

She leans on my kitchen counter and swirls her beer in front of her. I've never been intimidated by a woman before, but I have a strong inkling that Kelsey might whip my ass. "I was hoping you could tell me. At your father's event, you and Eli are trying to keep everyone from figuring out you took long hot showers together and the next thing I see is you two having a dark and uncomfortable moment, and he's been holed up in his office ever since. So what the actual fuck happened?"

The sick dread that's been curled in my belly since Davis showed me the story is stronger now, drawing all of me into myself, until my bones are pressing against my skin. I retrieve my phone and hand it to her. "My so-called fiancé is orchestrating this."

I say nothing as she reads the draft article.

She offers me that odd smile again as she looks up at me.

"Sucks getting your heart stomped on, doesn't it?"

The hurt is back, raw and aching and fundamentally *empty*. I try to speak but no sound comes out. I cover my mouth with my sweatshirt-covered hand. Shame crawls over my skin even as my eyes water.

In a million years, I never would have thought of Kelsey as someone I could lean on. Laugh with. Share a drink with.

I damn sure never expected her to put her arms around my shoulders and let me cry myself empty.

Again.

Eli

WHEN YOUR WORLD is going to shit, it generally helps to start drinking heavily. The trick is to remain intoxicated so that the shit storm looks all swirly and full of pretty colors. Or until you pass out and run out of fucks to give. Either option really works.

I left the party after Parker walked away from me. Left Deacon and Kelsey to clean everything up. I'm in the running for shittiest boss of the year award at the moment.

I am not nearly intoxicated enough for this shit.

I stare at the dark golden liquid in the glass as I hold it up to the light. "I guess they can say I gave it a good run."

My words are slurred. I'm pretty sure I'm about ninety percent in the bag. Which is not nearly far enough.

What the fuck was I thinking? The war was eventually going to follow me home. Why am I surprised that threats of being exposed for my part in it would hit at exactly the worst moment possible? I mean, I couldn't have *planned* a more perfectly terrible time for it to hit.

Guess that's what I get for thinking I was smart enough to deal with it when it happened. I should have known better.

I should have known someone like Parker would never understand. Her walking away stings in a cut-out-your-heart-and-stomp-on-it kind of way.

"You always drown your sorrows in a hundred-dollar bottle of whiskey?"

I squint at Deacon, glaring at me from the doorway. "Might as well enjoy it while it lasts." Because once that article runs, my business is getting flushed down the crapper. I raise my glass in a halfcocked attempt at showing him where my priorities are at the moment but it tips too far, sloshing some of the golden liquid onto a bill on my desk. "Hope that wasn't important."

The glass is halfway to my lips before I realize that I'm lifting an empty hand. My glass is floating toward the desk, and Deacon looks like he's ready to do some serious damage if I try to take it from him.

"Pretty sure your liver doesn't appreciate the jihad you've declared on it," he says. "Now what the fuck happened that you decided to leave me and Kelsey high and fucking dry?"

"Pretty sure that's none of your business," I mutter, sliding down in my chair and resting my head against the back. Jesus-tap dancing-Christ, I'm a mess. My entire fucking life is ending because I got tangled up with *her* and all I can think about is that she's gone.

"Actually, it is our business when our fucking boss decides not to come out of his office for twelve fucking hours." He frowns. "Where the hell have you been pissing? Never mind. I don't want to know."

"It was all bound to come out someday." I drag my hands over my face. I reach for the whiskey glass.

"Touch that fucking glass and I'll throw it against the goddamned wall."

And there goes my goddamned temper. "I'm not sure who the fuck you think you're talking to." I am in his face, toe to toe with him. In the time I've known him, we've never once gotten into it like this. Sucks that this is how things end. "I'll drink if I goddamned want to fucking drink."

And because the universe is testing my resolve, the glass shatters against the wall.

But it's not Deacon who throws it.

It's Parker, who's materialized out of fucking nowhere. And she looks as surprised about throwing it as I do. But I'm also not in the mood for any of her shit today, either. "Who the fuck let her in?"

"I let myself in." She looks ready for war.

"You can let yourself right back out again, sweetheart."

"I'm not going anywhere. This is happening because of me and I'm going to fix it."

She hands her phone to Deacon, distracting him away from the fight. He frowns as he stares at it for several seconds.

I sink back into my chair and snag the bottle of whiskey, dragging it to my lips while they're both distracted.

It's a long moment before he hands her phone back to her. "Well, that certainly is a clusterfuck." He breathes out hard and drags his hands through his hair. "Look, Captain Jack over here needs to sober up before we can do much of anything."

"I'll take him upstairs," Parker says quietly. "This is my fault. For once in my life, I'm going to stay and fix this."

"You ever babysit a drunk before?"

It's disconcerting to listen to them talk about me like I'm not sitting right there. Okay, maybe I'm no longer really sitting. More like listing to one side, but still.

"Yeah. Actually, I have." She lifts her chin. "You run the bar, keep things normal. I'll stay with him."

Deacon jerks his head toward her phone. "What do we do about that?"

"I'm not sure yet. I'll figure something out."

She doesn't sound confident. Neither does Deacon, for that

matter.

I don't offer anything. Better to contribute silence than the utter lack of hope that's a tight band around my chest.

I manage to stand, and reach across my desk to pat Deacon on the shoulder. "Thanks for bringing Sorority Barbie. But I don't need a babysitter."

"Now who's being a dick?" Deacon slips his arm around my waist to keep me from stumbling and guides me to the stairs that lead up to my apartment. "Go. Sober your ass up and let's figure this shit out." He grunts as we collide with the corner. And by we, I mean his shoulder. "I'm not quitting on you."

I press my lips into a flat line. "Thanks, man."

I trip up the first step as Deacon goes to run my bar, and Parker is there, breaking my fall with her shoulder, propping me up. "Come on. Don't break your neck."

It hurts, having her this close. Knowing how badly I fucked everything up.

Knowing that nothing I can say or do is going to fix anything between us. Hurting because just like everyone else in my life, she left when I didn't quite meet expectations.

I do the only thing that comes natural to guys like me.

"It's all a show for people like you, isn't it? Drag out the tattooed veteran. Fuck him for funsies. Then head back to your real life as the congressman's fiancée? Is that how this goes?"

Lashing out doesn't feel good, but it feels normal. It's so much easier than admitting how much it slays me to remember her walking away.

She fishes my keys out of my pocket and unlocks the apartment door.

"Being an asshole doesn't become you," she says mildly.

Next thing I know, I'm facedown on the couch where I first touched her, darkness swirling up around me to draw me down into the abyss.

And now I know what regret tastes like.

CHAPTER 28

Parker

THANKFULLY HE'S ASLEEP. I'm not sure I can handle any more verbal slaps. He's not a funny drunk, that's for sure, but I didn't expect him to hit below the belt. That *hurts*.

And it hurts sitting here, listening to his breathing, waiting for him to wake up. Hopefully sober. Hopefully ready to explain things in a way that makes sense.

A car passes beneath the apartment window. The light runs from one side of the apartment to the other before disappearing into the darkness outside.

Memories are colliding with reality. The last time I sat like this it was with Meaghan, the night she did a few too many pain pills.

I'd had no one to call that night, either.

I rest my head on my knees, pulling them up against my chest. Painful words fill the silence but it's better than the hollow beating of my heart.

"You know, I didn't really know what I was getting into when I signed up for the job. I wanted to learn about The Pint. I wanted to write a great report for my thesis." I close my eyes. "I was so damn happy to get the internship with you, and you never had a clue. You thought it was just because I wanted to sleep with you." My chest tightens. "You've never thought much of me. Of girls like me. No one does." I suck in a hard breath, trying to dislodge the ball of ice around my heart. "You look at me and see some empty-headed Barbie." I close my eyes. "I thought you were different."

There's a quiet knock on the apartment door and I get up to open it. Kelsey is standing there holding a plate of cheese fries and two beers. "Figured I'd come keep you company."

"Aren't you supposed to be helping Deacon with the bar?"

"He's roped in some of the other guys for help tonight. Besides, it's Thursday." Thursdays are usually pretty quiet.

I take one of the beers and let her in. We settle at the small kitchen counter. "These are quite possibly the best cheese fries I've ever had."

Kelsey grins and takes a pull off her beer. "It's the sadness. It makes everything bad for you taste better."

"I thought that was hunger."

"Nope. Sadness is the best flavoring for all the salt, sugar, and fatty things that are slowly killing us all."

I raise my beer. "Here's to a slow death, covered in melted cheese and bacon."

Our beers clink together, and the silence descends again. "So Eli has this really bizarre ability to find us."

"'Us'?"

"Vets. Former soldiers, mostly. It's like we've got some weird homing beacon that draws us into The Pint." She stares down at the cheese fries. "He's saved more than one of our lives. Just by giving us the space to figure out who we are without the uniform. But by being there, too."

"Did he save yours?"

"Mine's still up for grabs. Death hasn't decided if she wants me yet or not." She glances down at her forearms like the tattoos belong to someone else. Then she smiles up at me, the flash of sadness gone. "And *that's* a little emo, given the current situation." She scrapes some of the cheese off the plate with one of the remaining fries. "So what are you thinking about with regard to the Eli situation?" she finally asks.

"You know this is really about me, don't you?" I ask quietly.

Kelsey lifts one brow. "What gave it away?"

I rub the beer against my forehead. "My fiancé is using this article as leverage. He wants me home, away from this place. If I don't do what he says, he's going to ruin everyone's life."

Kelsey raises her beer in mock salute. "Nice boyfriend you've got there."

I smile flatly. "Yeah, well, any doubts I was having have been reified into full-blown anxiety attacks."

"I guess I don't understand why he wants you that badly? I mean, no offense or anything, but this is a little stalker-esque."

"My dad is a powerful defense contractor. They'd be better off marrying each other but instead, I get caught in the middle of their alliance building."

"Survivor: Marriage Market, huh?"

"You have a great way of making things seem less serious than they are."

"It's a gift."

I scrape a piece of cheese off the plate. "You know, despite all this, I can't wrap my brain around the accusations in that thing."

Kelsey taps one red-tipped nail on the table. "You know the official report says Eli was investigated and cleared of any wrong-doing, right? His men shot some prisoners. He sent up the report as soon as he suspected something wasn't right."

I shake my head. "If he did the right thing, why does the article make him look like a monster instead of a hero? How can it twist the facts so much?"

"Because it's all about drawing inferences and letting people make their own conclusions. Propaganda 101." She takes another pull off the beer. "Most people don't read beyond the headlines. Congressman's fiancée tied to war criminal. Pretty hard to get beyond that, even if you do read the whole article." She points the beer at me. "Case in point. You know who General McChrystal is?"

"He's the guy who got fired in Afghanistan, right?"

"I'm actively impressed that you knew *anything* about him, but your answer is exactly what I'm talking about. He wasn't fired; he resigned. And he resigned because of things his men were saying, not things he actually said or did. But all everyone remembers is 'he's the guy who got fired'."

"Then it doesn't matter what we do. Davis wants me back. He's given me a day to say my goodbyes. If I don't, Eli is going to be dragged through the mud, all because I worked here." I lower my head to my forearms. "Fuck me."

"I'm pretty sure that's what got you into this mess." I lift my head and glare at her. "What, too soon?"

I smile because I can't help it. And I might cry if I don't. "Definitely too soon."

I drum my nails on the barrel of my beer bottle. Turning the label around, I inspect the logo, the colors. "Not your father's stout." I frown, reading it again.

"What are you thinking?"

"The marketing. Not your father's stout. This beer is positioning itself against something old but something that matters to people. Their fathers and their fathers' stouts."

"So? Eli isn't a beer." She pushes away from the table. "Talking about beer isn't going to fucking fix this, Parker."

I shove aside the hurt. I'll deal with that later. "We need to wake Eli up. I've got an idea."

Eli groans and sits up. "I'm not interested in your ideas." He sits up like he's moving through water and his body's weighted down.

"Too bad. You're going to hear them."

Kelsey's face blanches white and she skirts away from the table and closer to the door. "I'll just let you two get this out of your system." She mouths what looks like *good luck* and slides her index finger into a loop made by her other index finger and thumb. I'm pretty sure we're not even close to makeup sex yet.

If we ever will be.

It's hard to be irritated with her for abandoning me. I don't know what Kelsey did in her past life, but right then I am utterly grateful for whatever powers that be that have put her in my life as a friend.

I just hope that will continue after this.

"I was willing to listen a few days ago. Now, I'm getting ready to put my liver through a hazing event, if you don't mind."

"Yeah, I do mind." I sit on the table in front of him, physically blocking him from the whiskey bottle behind me.

There is fury in his eyes. "This isn't a fucking game, Parker." His low words are laced with anger and hurt. I should be afraid but I'm not. I know he won't hurt me. He would never hurt me.

Which is why I'm not afraid to go toe to toe with him.

"You know what? You're right. It's not a fucking game and screw you for thinking I would trivialize this." The hurt is a physical thing, clawing at my skin, slicing at me until I am raw and wounded but I won't step away. I won't retreat.

He shakes his head, reaching around me for the whiskey bottle. He looks up at me. If we weren't in the middle of a shit-show, it would be so easy to slide my fingers through his hair. To slip into his lap and open for him and lose myself in his touch.

It would be easier if he would just lash out. But this quiet disapproval is the worst kind of suffering.

He shakes his head, letting the bottle dangle between his index finger and thumb. "You sit there and you judge me the entire time you're trying to convince me otherwise. You've never had to make the decisions I made. The choices. The fucking regret. The hardest thing you'll ever do is decide whether to break away from

Daddy's money and live your own fucking life. I did that already. Got the motherfucking t-shirt. I walked away from everything because of that day. And I never looked back."

Somehow, the conversation has twisted to me. I did not see that coming but in an instant, I'm on the defensive. "You think it's so easy for me to walk away from my entire life?"

"As opposed to letting a man you don't love fuck you and hurt you and treat you like you're his own personal Barbie doll? Yeah, I fucking do."

"It's so goddamned easy for you, isn't it? With your moral clarity?"

"When *you* have to make life-and-death decisions, come talk to me about moral clarity."

I refuse to let him box me out. "You don't get to make this about me. This is one hundred percent not about me."

"Oh really? Your name linked to an alleged war criminal isn't about you? Spare me, princess."

"Don't call me that."

"Why? You are. You're just some spoiled business school pedigree sorority girl slumming before she settles down to something respectable. I know all about your type."

"You don't know anything about me. Or the decisions I made just to survive." My eyes are burning, the air locked in my lungs, refusing to release.

"Then why the fuck are you so furious about a hit piece filled with lies?"

"Because it says you're a fucking war criminal! And even though I've got a pretty good imagination, I can't really match the you standing in front of me with the you I read about in that article."

"That's because that article wants you and the rest of the country to think exactly that." He lifts the bottle of whiskey to his lips. He takes another drink. "The investigation cleared me of all wrongdoing, but I didn't know what was going on in my unit, either." His words are quiet now, laced with regret and recrimination. "A commander is responsible for everything his unit does or fails to do." His slurred words are muffled and bitter. "I failed in my most basic responsibility as an officer. My commander protected me. It made me sick to think that he would protect me, allow me to advance, when I hadn't known what was going on in my own formation." He sighs heavily and pushes up off the couch. "So I resigned. As soon as we got back to the States, I resigned my commission. I took off my West Point ring, and I walked away from everything. I couldn't do it anymore. They protected me knowing I'd screwed up."

Finally, he looks me in the eye. The bitterness in his gaze is darker than the deepest abyss. "I am the man in that article. I'm the commander who didn't lead his men. I'm the commander who didn't see what was going on around me until it was too late."

I rise and move toward him.

He stops me. "Don't." That single word might as well be a physical barrier.

I take another step closer. "You don't get to call the shots here." I stop right in front of him. Slip the bottle from his hands and thread my fingers with his. "You told me once to take the leap. To trust you." I lift my mouth to his, brushing my lips across his. "I can fix this. I can help you."

He turns away from me, stumbling toward his small bedroom. "I don't want your help."

I let him go. Allowing him space.

I leave his apartment, letting the door close quietly behind me. "Too bad," I say to the closed door.

CHAPTER 29

Eli

Six hours later, I stumble down to my office. There's a quiet rap on my office door. I look up, hoping to see Parker standing there in her yoga pants and a sweater.

But instead it's Deacon. "Try not to look so disappointed that it's me," he mumbles. "You know you could try calling her. There's this amazing thing called modern technology. Fascinating stuff."

I can feel the enamel in my teeth chip from grinding my teeth so hard.

Thankfully, he lets it go. "There's a reporter here to see you. Ryan Pool? Says he spoke to your publicist and set up an interview." Deacon leans against the doorframe. "When did you hire a publicist?"

"I don't have one. Tell him to fuck off."

"Can't do that. Turns out, he was a public affairs officer in his former life and he's here to help you unfuck the shitshow PR disaster your company command has become."

"You know, in the real world, everybody and their fucking brother isn't a soldier or a former soldier."

"Yeah well, in our world, we live an hour and a half from Fort Bragg. I would expect we'd have more than our share of soldiers floating around." He frowns. "Do you really want me to wax intellectual about why there are so many soldiers gravitating to the space you've created here?"

"Not really." I try to give him the hint that I need him to leave but, typical Deacon, he's decided to be a pain in the ass.

Again.

"Ryan Pool is not the antichrist," he says quietly. "Maybe he's worth talking to."

"Never say never."

"Yeah, well, I just spent an hour drinking with him and he seems like a pretty straightforward guy." He swears softly. "You know, you don't have to be a belligerent asshole about everything. Fucking let someone else make a goddamned decision." He glares at me then. "Talk. To the fucking. Reporter."

I slam the lid down on my laptop and instantly regret it. I hope I haven't managed to crack the glass. "Now isn't the time, Deac."

"Now is absolutely the fucking time. You're holed up in here like some kind of hobbit, mourning the loss of his one twue wuv."

I glance at him sideways. "Did you just make a *Princess Bride* reference?"

"Maybe. Go talk to the fucking guy."

"I hate reporters."

"Don't care. Tell your story or someone else will. You've let fear of this article trap you. You need to get this shit stopped, time now."

In his former life, Deacon was an NCO. I never could see it before, but in that moment, with him barking an order at me and pointing toward my bar, I can finally see the fierce sergeant he must have been once upon a time.

I say nothing, walk into my bar. The reporter is sitting in one of the small booths, typing away at a laptop that looks like it's several replacement cycles past its prime.

He does not look like the antichrist. Or maybe he is. He's smooth, standing and offering his hand. "Thanks for finally agreeing to meet with me."

I swallow and sit, ignoring the proffered hand. I feel dirty sitting at a table in the bar that I built. It's empty now except for us and Deacon, who is behind the bar ostensibly working on the prep for tonight's opening but in reality just watching my back.

"I'm not sure what questions I can answer that you don't already know," I say quietly.

He drops his hand and looks a little put out. He recovers quickly, though, and continues typing on his laptop. "I learned about your case in grad school. It's easy to understand why your men did what they did. But I wanted to know what it meant for you. For the man who was supposed to lead them. How you sleep at night?"

I smile flatly. "I run a bar. Sleeping isn't really my primary concern."

"Yeah, I can see that." He jots something down on his notepad. "I want to run this as a human-interest story. My editor is really interested in seeing more pieces about this sort of thing."

"You have an editor who is willing to pay for human-interest stories? What, are you funded by a secret billionaire benefactor?"

Pool grins. "I don't ask those kinds of questions."

"No, you just ask people to bare their souls."

"The best of us do."

"For what?" I swallow a hard knot in my throat. "For what?"

"We need stories." He hesitates for a long moment. "Because they're what makes us human."

His words take a moment to penetrate, settling over me like a warm blanket. "You were in Iraq."

"Army. I served in Mosul in 2009 as a lieutenant with 3rd Brigade, First Cav."

I smile then. "I was part of 5th Brigade. Death Dealers." Each brigade in the Cav has a mascot. First Brigade was Ironhorse. Second was Blackjack. Third was Greywolf. My brigade was the Death Dealers, my company, the Wolfpack. The sense of belonging is almost instantaneous. "We chewed a lot of the same dirt at Hood."

"We did." He closes his laptop lid. "Look, I'm not here to ask you the whys or the whats. I want my readers to understand what it's like to command men who have done terrible things at war."

I look up at him. Trying to keep the frustration from leaking back in. "Everything we do at war is a terrible thing. Every house we destroy. Every dog we kill. Every child whose father we imprison. There is nothing good about war."

"And yet, I'm willing to bet you'd trade it all to go back. Just for one day."

I shake my head. "I have everything I need here." Except one thing.

"It's not the same, you know that. You know it's different downrange."

"It is. And yeah, I miss some of the stupid stuff. But I've…I've got the bar. And the gang who hang out and work here."

"Is it enough?"

"Yeah. Yeah, man, it is. What I do here matters."

He looks at me then. "You're a West Pointer, aren't you?"

"I was."

"You don't sound proud of that. You weren't like every other cadet at West Point? Eager to go? Eager to prove yourself? To test yourself in battle?"

I look down at my hands. At my empty ring finger where my class ring used to be. It hasn't been there in more than half a decade. "I took my class ring off the day I decided I was no longer a soldier." I chew on my bottom lip for a moment. Selecting my words carefully. "I wanted to be like the men I was raised to believe in. Heroes who were honest and loyal and true." I look up at him. "I still believe that real leaders are those things. But when I wasn't punished for what my men did, I felt...dirty. Like I was being given a pass for not doing my job."

"But if you didn't know, why should you be held responsible for what they did?" His question is carefully measured.

"Because I was raised to believe that leaders are responsible for everything their soldiers do, or fail to do. I was basically absolved of that responsibility. To keep me in the fight."

"And you feel this was unfair?"

I nod. "I know it doesn't make sense. No one wants to be punished. But I wanted to be held to the same standard. I needed to believe in what we said was the right way to live."

"So you're an idealist?"

"I was. I'm not anymore."

"What are you now?"

"A cynic. Maybe. A pragmatist. I'm not sure."

"Maybe you're just looking for something to believe in. Maybe we all are." He slides his laptop toward me.

It's open to an article on the *New York Times* At War Blog:

More to the Story: Beyond the Dangerous Veteran Stereotype

By Parker Hauser.

I say nothing, my throat blocked.

And I start to read.

Parker

I'VE MOSTLY PICKED myself up. And by that, I mean I've showered and gotten food and withdrawn my application for the executive management program.

I haven't actually opened my laptop and done the formal paperwork yet, but I've notified Professor Blake that I will not be applying for the executive management program. But hey, ideas are the first step to action, right?

I'm meeting Davis for lunch. In a public place, which is good because that means there will be no scenes.

He's not exactly happy about my op-ed in the *New York Times*. Add in the article that Ryan Pool sent to the AP that managed to get ahead of Davis's article.

I've out maneuvered him. He's going to be less than pleased.

Which is also part of the reason I've gone silent on all communications. I turned off all my social media notifications and considered deleting all of it. Ignored calls from media outlets, wanting to know more about the personal side of Eli. A TV tabloid offered me fifty thousand dollars for an exclusive tell all.

But the best part about the whole scenario is that Ryan's piece makes *Davis* look fantastic. Like the up-and-coming congressman is going to be actively involved in working on issues at Veterans Affairs. That he's fully supporting his fiancée's desire to be more involved in Veterans' issues, too.

He's going to be so pissed he lost control of the narrative.

Today, he's going to lose any control he had left.

I walk into the restaurant precisely on time. I'm never early. Never late. I know my role here, and I will play it well.

Because this is the last time.

I'm not sure how I'll manage but I'm going to figure it out. I may have lost everything that mattered to me, but in the brief time that Eli and The Pint were part of my life, I had a taste of something I'd forgotten existed: possibility.

Davis looks up when I walk in. He stands, offers me a cold kiss on my cheek.

I'm finally pissed but I smile pleasantly. I'm pissed that my so-called fiancé was going to ruin a good man's life just to get back at me. Pissed that my father has gone silent again, once he figured out that Davis and I were most likely permanently ending things.

Pissed at everything and everyone who is supposed to matter in my life that turned their back on me and walked away. Again.

"You think you're so smart, don't you?"

"Hello to you, too," I say, a pleasant smile pasted on my face.

His eyes flash but in the soft restaurant lighting, you'd have to be paying attention to catch it.

I'm paying attention.

"Now is not the time to get lippy."

"When is a good time?" I ask sweetly, still smiling. Remember to play the part. Play by his rules.

He waits until I lift the water glass to my lips. "Are you proud of your little op-ed? Does it ease your guilt for fucking around on me?"

I lower the glass. "Believe it or not, everything doesn't revolve around you, Davis."

His eyes flash dangerously and he sets his own glass down a little too hard. "That's where you're wrong. This was always about you humiliating me. Do you know how weak it makes me look that you were fucking around at a pathetic bar?"

I can feel the rage building in my chest once again. I swallow three ice chips to try and dislodge it from my lungs. I need to think clearly here. "Maybe it's time you look in the mirror. You were going to run that article, deliberately framed in a way that ruined Eli's life. It made him look complicit in the murder of civilians."

He smirks. "You're taking this too personally. I just wanted to get you away from him. Back where you belong."

It's difficult to explain the emotions pressing on my lungs right now. Fear. Panic. Adrenaline as I step to the edge of the precipice that leads to the rest of my life.

"Well it looks like you lose. This relationship is not going to work."

His eyes flicker in surprise. Which is actively shocking. "I'm sorry?"

He honestly didn't see this coming? "We'll do it quietly. Let the excitement from this op-ed die down. You'll issue a statement saying we've grown apart, on a Friday afternoon in the middle of the summer. Maybe during Shark Week so no one will notice."

"Is this still about the bruises?" He sinks back into his chair. "You're overreacting. That kind of thing happens all the time."

"You accused me of cheating because one of my father's friends sent me a dick pic. I think I have a right to be upset," I say mildly. It's amazing how little I care about this conversation. I just want it to be over. To be away from him.

"I'm sorry I didn't believe you. Does that help?"

"No, it doesn't."

His words, his attitude just reinforce how much I don't matter to him. How I never will. His apology is a means to an end. Nothing genuine. Nothing sincere.

How did I ever want attention from this man? It doesn't matter. He doesn't matter. And that's what's irritating him.

I'm letting him go. He has no control here. No power.

And it's finally dawning on him.

It's a powerful feeling.

I set my napkin down on my plate. "There's really nothing more to say. We're done, Davis."

He shrugs and tries to look like he doesn't care. But he does. "I guess so. You have my secretary's number if you need to get in touch. I'll expect you to return the ring."

I smile at him and I am sure my expression is positively blinding. "I've already sold it and donated the money to charity." I push my chair back from the table. "Thank you for this little talk."

I leave quickly. I need to get away from the tight pressure in my chest. As though there's some part of me, deep down, that had held on to the hope that someday he would look at me and see me, really see me and tell me that I mattered.

But I don't. And I don't think I ever did. To him, at least.

The only person in this world that I ever really mattered to died when my mom died.

I'm not sure where I'm going. But I'm not staying here one second longer.

I'm free.

So why does it feel like my soul is lost, with nowhere to go?

CHAPTER 30

Eli

THERE'S a storm on the horizon. The kind of storm that sends people scurrying for cover and weathermen sending out emergency alerts.

It's the kind of storm one should not be out walking in. But there I am, standing in front of Parker's building, trying to find the courage to walk up the stairs and knock on her door.

I've never really thought of myself as a coward before, but there you have it.

I have no idea what I'm going to say. What I can say that will make things right.

I rub my hand over my face and push out a deep breath. "Okay, I can do this."

"You know, it's never really a good sign to stand around talking to yourself."

I didn't hear her approach but now she's all I can see as she walks toward me along the brick sidewalk, and does it with fucking grace and style in her three-inch heels.

"Desperate times and all that." God, I sound like I'm about to cry. I offer a half-assed smile instead. "It turns out I have a publicist I didn't know about."

She tips her head but doesn't smile. "I read the article Ryan wrote. He did a good job."

"I'm pretty sure I've never been so glad one of my employees has been asked for a blowjob in all my life."

She laughs quietly. "Yeah, well, we got lucky he wasn't actually a sexually harassing scumbag." She clears her throat. "I mean, your publicist is lucky."

I take a single step closer. "How did you…?"

She doesn't back away but she doesn't move in, either. There is a chasm between us, a gulf that I created.

"You should know that Davis was never going to run the article," she says softly. "He was using it to threaten me. To get me to run home." She swallows. "I might have. But he threatened you. And Kelsey and Deacon. And I…I couldn't let him do that. Couldn't let him hurt you because of me." She rubs her hands over her arms. The pressure in the atmosphere is dropping rapidly. "I took a risk. I was terrified but I figured if Ryan wouldn't help then we really had nothing to lose."

I want to pull her close, to protect her from the rain, from everything.

But I don't have the right to touch her. I failed her. When she needed me most, I stumbled and let her fall all by herself.

"I was coming to see you." It's then that I notice: she looks… lost. Everything I was going to say…none of that matters now. "What happened?"

"You don't have to pretend to care about me anymore, Eli." There is utter sadness in those words. "I know I'm not one of yours."

She moves to step past me.

I stand there, rooted to the spot, the realization that she is once more walking away hammering inside my brain.

I don't think. I grab her then, turning her toward me, my hands rough on her shoulders.

"I never pretended." It's everything I can do not to rail at her. "Everything between us was always real."

She slips her hands between our bodies, pushing against my chest. "Don't. Okay? I can't take any more right now." She smiles sadly and I let her go.

Because I have to give her what she wants.

Even if it's not what she needs.

"What happened?"

Her lips press together in a flat, humorless line. "I'm free. I broke things off with Davis. No more political parties. No more fundraisers." She looks away. "My father is pissed. I don't think I'm even expected home for the holidays anymore." Her voice cracks a little. And shatters my heart.

"I thought that's what you wanted."

"I thought so, too." Her bottom lip quivers and she bites down on it hard enough that I wince in sympathy. "It hurts. Knowing that you don't really matter after all."

I move into her space and gather her closer, drawing her near until her cheek is pressed to my heart, her body molded to mine.

She doesn't resist. She stays still for a moment, then she sinks into me.

It is a moment of perfect pleasure. Not sexual. Not erotic. Just the pure sensation of touching another person. Of full, deep, human connection.

I half expect her to ask me to leave, and I will, if she asks. I won't force her. That's what started this whole shitshow to begin with. No one was willing to listen to what she wanted.

Instead, I cup her face, because I can't not touch her. "You matter, Parker," I whisper. "You matter so fucking much it hurts."

"It hurts."

The rejection in those two little words slices through any defenses. I rest my cheek on her head and squeeze my eyes closed, ashamed of how I hurt her. Of how I created this mess. "From the minute I met you, I wanted you. I wanted to know what made you tick." I brush my lips across hers. "But I couldn't let myself get close." I lower my forehead to hers. "I was afraid of what I felt for you. Of how alive I felt around you." My eyes are wet. "It's hard for me to trust people."

"Everyone around you trusts you."

"They're supposed to depend on me. Not the other way around." Her hands are warm on my chest, right over my heart, that's beating just for her. "I didn't know how to trust you. I didn't want to. And when you walked away after the article, I thought I was right to not trust you." I breathe in sharply, trying to yank everything back in and failing miserably. "I'm here to grovel. To beg for your forgiveness." I brush my lips against hers once more. "I've been lost without you. There's this Parker-shaped hole in my life that whiskey won't fill."

She smiles sadly. "You've tried?"

"I've tried." I pull her close. "Then my liver went on strike and decided I had to do whatever it took to get you to come back." I cup her face again. "I'm so fucking sorry. For everything. For not trusting you. For hurting you. For not being man enough to love you the way you deserve to be loved."

Her arms finally slide around my waist. "Well, seeing how I wanted to be loved up against a brick wall in an alley the night we met, I'd say you're definitely more than the right man."

I laugh and pull her close, needing the contact, the reassurance that this is real. That I'm standing there holding her and she's making jokes and my life isn't coming crashing down around me.

"Can we start again?"

"What, you want me to get drunk and walk into your bar and ask you to fuck me in the alley? I think that ship has sailed." She threads her arms around my neck. "But my apartment is just up those stairs. I'll warn you, I've been a little messy lately. There may be unmentionables on the floor."

Still laughing, I kiss her deeply, lifting her and carrying her inside.

It's as close to forgiveness as I'll come in this lifetime.

EPILOGUE

Parker

"Is it always this busy on Tuesdays?"

Kelsey grins at me and hands me an empty bottle. "Since your marketing plan is working like fucking genius, we're twice as busy as normal. Be a dear. I need another Laphroaig."

"That's the second one tonight."

"Tell that to the alcoholic business school party over there. They're stress-testing their black card tonight."

I grin. "That takes a lot of money."

"You should see their tab," she tells me. "Go. I need that bottle."

I've been at The Pint for almost six months now. It's been a lifetime since the article ran in the *New York Times* about the commander of a company accused of war crimes.

It had remarkably less legs than we feared. It didn't even make the most-read articles for a day.

I walk through the stacked cases of whiskey, looking for the Laphroaig for Kelsey.

I know the moment I am not alone. I can feel him, standing behind me, his body dark and warm, his breath hot on my neck.

It has become somewhat of a game, how long he can go with keeping his hands off me.

"You know this skirt drives me crazy." His words are rough on my skin, and I am already slick and aching for his touch.

I make a noise in my throat and shift, spreading my legs a little, bracing my hands on the shelf in front of me.

"It's amazing how little self-control you have these days." I arch my back, grinding my hips against his. He is rigid beneath his pants, more than ready.

He slips his hand over my belly, down, lower, until he cups my sex, squeezing gently. "Pot, meet kettle." He pinches me gently through the thin material of my skirt.

It takes him another moment to realize what's missing. "Holy shit. You're not wearing any panties."

I drop my head back to his shoulder, still rubbing my ass against his cock. "Hello, Captain Obvious."

"Are you serious? Right now?" He's still stroking me, inching the skirt up higher with each little movement. Then he touches me, his fingers coated in my wetness. "Jesus, you're wet."

"Please." I'm just this side of begging. "I want this. I want you. Right now." I've been learning what I like. What feels good with him.

I'm still in awe at the sheer pleasure his touch strikes inside me. I still brace each time but it's less now and each time, he fills me with the sweetest pleasure. Never pain.

He is a patient lover.

I want to test that patience. I want him unrestrained. Wild. I want all of him. I reach behind me, releasing his cock from his pants. Even at this angle, just touching him makes me ache to have him inside me.

He strokes me again, his fingers sliding through my flesh. I urge him closer, arching until he is there, just there.

He drops his head to my shoulder, fighting, restraining his motions. Inching inside me in a thousand small pulses.

I push back, urging him deeper, taking him fully inside me in a single movement. I suck in a breath as he is there, pushed up against me, filling me—tight, and sweet and hard inside me.

"Did…does it…"

"No. It…just move. Please. Jesus, I need you."

He slips from my body and every nerve is on fire as he fills me once more.

"It's good. So good."

His arms are tight around me, holding me where he needs me, holding me against him as he fills me, again and again up against the bottles of expensive whiskey. Higher and higher my body clenches, needing the motion, the speed of him pushing into me. Harder, faster, until I shatter, flying apart and trying to muffle the sound against my own forearm.

His cheek is pressed to mine, his fingers still stroking me gently, like a master tuning an instrument that plays only for him. "I could get used to this," he whispers against my ear.

I smile, purring with satisfaction and the echoes of pleasure that are humming through my body. "I certainly hope so."

He is still deep inside me as he takes my left hand and presses something cold onto my ring finger.

My breath is locked in my throat. "Eli."

"Shh." He nips my ear as he slips the ring further onto my finger. "I'm asking. Not telling. Not demanding." He threads his fingers with mine. "I want to be able to touch you for the rest of my life. I want to go to sleep, no matter where I am in the world, and know that you're there. That you're mine."

I pull our joined hands to my heart. "This angle makes it a little difficult for jumping into your arms."

He slips from my body and turns me, lifting me until our bodies are close again and I can feel him hard against me once more. "Is that a yes?"

I twine my arms around his neck. "Yeah. That's a yes."

"Then I can die happy."

"Please don't. I really didn't plan on that 'rest of my life' thing coming to fruition tonight."

He pulls me close and laughs.

And everything in my world is perfect.

Keep reading for an uncorrected first look at CATCH MY FALL, coming 2017.

CATCHY MY FALL

Deacon

"Can I touch it?"

Sweet baby Jesus, the things I do for my job. The girl leaning across the bar is about one deep breath away from bursting out of her top and every red-blooded man in the joint is hoping for just that.

She leans over a little further and runs her finger over the chain tattooed into my skin around my neck. Not a thick chain like a collar or hand cuffs. No, the chain is a thin line of silver balls, pieced together to represent the real chain I no longer wear.

The dog tag tattoo was the first thing I did when I joined the Army and it was the stuff that NCOs laugh at privates for doing. I damn sure laughed at my joes when they did stupid shit like I did once upon a time.

She smells like oranges and sunshine and a little too much Patron. I lean closer, in part to do my service to mankind and keep her from actually falling out of that top. Eli tends to frown on public nudity. The cops don't really like getting called for those kinds of things.

They like bar fights even less and naked chicks tend to spark the caveman in even the most civilized of hipster college dude.

So it's part of my duty description to help Ms. Patron keep her clothes on.

Her finger is soft and smooth against my skin as she traces the small chain. Over the ridge of my collarbone until it disappears into the white t-shirt I've worn to work tonight.

The trace of her skin over mine is addictive. I want to lean closer to let her press her lips to my skin and see what else she'd like to do with that perfectly painted mouth.

It's no sacrifice to stand perfectly still while her fingers trace over my skin. Her touch is a connection, pure human connection linking me from the alcohol-induced haze to the world of sensual touch.

It's not an easy thing to break the contact but I do. Because what I need will not be satisfied in a simple touch. "Another drink?"

She leans back and traces the same finger over her bottom lip. Christ she's going to make me ask her for her number.

"I'm trying to behave," she whispers. "But yeah, I think another shot would be just the thing."

"You misbehave often?" Because I can't quite help myself.

"A little too often, to be honest."

"Why do you sound like that's a bad thing? Everyone's allowed to misbehave. Isn't that the fun of being an adult?"

She knocks back the shot and smiles at me, licking her lip. "I'm trying to pretend I'm not an adult tonight."

"Well, I'm not into daddy fetishes." I grin and wink at her, taking the sting of rejection out of my words. She wants to keep drinking, she can but I have to see to other customers.

It's Ranger Panty night. Which I'm honestly not sure how I feel about half the bar population running around in those shorts made infamous by the Rangers at Fort Benning.

Course, half the women in the bar are wearing them, too, which makes it really fucking hard to concentrate every time someone decides to bend over.

And dear god in heaven, thank you for the women who decided tonight was laundry night.

"You're drooling." Kelsey Ryder doesn't even blink as she reaches across me for the Patron bottle.

She has no idea what the sight of the lotus tattoo on her lower back does to me. And I'll never tell her.

I lost that chance in the bleeding deserts of Iraq.

I look away and focus on the here and now of pouring drinks and pretending we never knew each other before we both started working at The Pint.

"So are you." She pats my cheek like I'm some kind of neutered puppy.

"Yeah, well, I would say you're welcome but I'm not sure Eli is happy with the results of tonight's special event." Kelsey tosses back her own shot before pouring a line of twelve shots, all in a row.

"Why would he be upset? This shit is practically printing money."

Eli is the owner of The Pint and sometimes, he's fucking weird. Like tonight, for example.

Half the crowd is wearing Vineyard Vines and Sperrys. The other half is literally wearing combat boots and Ranger Panties. There is some mixing but for the most part, the military folks are on one side of the bar, laughing and getting tanked and the college crowd are doing an ethnography of military bar stories, watching warily from a distance, like they're afraid one of the vets is going to snap and shoot the place up.

This is fine, I'm sure. Like what could possibly go wrong?

As long as no one calls someone else a fucking moron, we should be okay.

But it's a bar. And despite our efforts, there is a schism down the middle of our space, one that I'm not sure how to heal.

Technically, it's not my job to heal anything. That's Eli. Everyone's favorite Boy Scout who looks like a Hell's Angel.

Unlike me, who looks like an angel and raises holy hell whenever I get the urge.

The music shifts from something pulsing and intense to smooth country.

And this is how our night ends, ladies and gentlemen.

In the middle of a bar fight about what music should be played, Kelsey shuffles into the space between the combatants and starts to dance.

And I mean really dance.

Her hips sway to the music, her eyes close. Her lips part just a little.

Enough to lure one of the Sperrys to move in behind her, his hand sliding down her hip, his body moving in sync with hers like they've done this before. Her tank slides higher, revealing the ink that spreads out around her waist.

It's enthralling, watching her move. Watching her lose herself in the feel of someone else's body against hers, the smooth slide of his hands down her flesh, drawing her closer.

I'm not the only one captured by the erotic duo. The smooth slow country continues and slowly, the tension in the bar dissipates, replaced by sensual energy from people daring to cross the gap and make that most elemental human connection.

And I feel suddenly, starkly, alone.

Just like always.

A MESSAGE FROM JESSICA SCOTT

Dear Reader,

Thank you so much for reading. If you'd like to make sure you never miss a new release, sign up for my newsletter at http://jessicascott.net/subscribe/ and please like my Facebook page at https://www.facebook.com/JessicaScottAuthor/. You can also join my reader room, affectionately known as The Pint for sneak peeks, giveaways and general all around shenanigans.

If you enjoyed the story, please consider leaving a review. Word of mouth is incredibly important for helping other readers discover new authors. I appreciate any and all reviews (whether positive or negative or somewhere in between).

Until next time!
Jess

ABOUT THE AUTHOR

Jessica Scott is an Iraq war veteran, an active duty army officer and the USA Today bestselling author of novels set in the heart of America's Army. She is the mother of two daughters, three cats and three dogs, and wife to a retired NCO.

She's also written for the New York Times At War Blog, PBS Point of View Regarding War, and IAVA. She deployed to Iraq in 2009 as part of Operation Iraqi Freedom (OIF)/New Dawn and has had the honor of serving as a company commander at Fort Hood, Texas twice.

She holds a Ph.D. in morality in Sociology with Duke University and she's been featured as one of Esquire Magazine's Americans of the Year for 2012.

Photo: Courtesy of Buzz Covington Photography

www.ingramcontent.com/pod-product-compliance
Lightning Source LLC
Chambersburg PA
CBHW050511190726
48284CB00003B/777